THE
SCHOOL
TRIP

BOOKS BY MIRANDA SMITH

THE
SCHOOL
TRIP

MIRANDA SMITH

bookouture

Published by Bookouture in 2023

An imprint of Storyfire Ltd.
Carmelite House
50 Victoria Embankment
London EC4Y 0DZ

www.bookouture.com

ISBN: 978-1-83790-056-5
eBook ISBN: 978-1-83790-055-8

This book is a work of fiction. Names, characters, businesses, organizations,
places and events other than those clearly in the public domain, are either the
product of the author's imagination or are used fictitiously. Any resemblance
to actual persons, living or dead, events or locales is entirely coincidental.

For Christopher

ONE

I have a plan.

Dr. Meade says you can't go through life without a plan, and she's been in school twice as long as I ever was. She's still learning. I know because she writes papers and when they're good enough, she gets to go talk about them at fancy schools.

She even wrote one about me.

Anyway, Dr. Meade knows her stuff, and she says everyone who wants to live a productive life must have a plan. Five-year. Month-long. Even a daily schedule can help. It's helped me.

For so long, I kept thinking about my life as a series of wins and losses. Dr. Meade says that isn't healthy. Sometimes I think she just says that because my losses are so overwhelming. If I kept thinking about them, I'd hurt myself again...

There's a lot about my past I wish I could change. A lot about me I wish I could change.

For the plan to work, I first had to admit the truth about myself. Then, I had to come to terms with what I really needed. The last part—let me tell you, this one is a doozy to get right—was figuring out how to make it happen.

All of it has led me to this point, to today's Step One: Take the girl.

TWO

EMMA

She's gone.

My eyes flit from the bus, back to the line of children, searching for her familiar silhouette, her hair, icy blonde and teased into a high ponytail. There are two dozen other children about her height and stature, all wearing the same burnt-orange shirt, but none of them are her.

Paranoia spikes. Chilly fear climbs my spine, branching out through my arms and legs, a vigilant frost. I must find her.

"Claire?" I call out, my voice rising above the cacophony of little voices around me. I'm starting to panic now. It's been, what? Thirty seconds? Sixty? How long has she been out of my sight?

"Claire?"

"Looking for someone?"

It's Laura Bailey, my fellow teacher. Mid-sixties with short gray hair, wearing the same orange shirt as the rest of the crowd. Her voice is calm and friendly, and soon I see why. Claire is standing behind her.

The kettle of emotions disperses, swiftly replaced with

relief, and more than that, embarrassment. It was only a moment of having her out of my sight. No reason to be alarmed.

"Why aren't you with the rest of your class?" I say, bending down to be at eye level with my six-year-old daughter.

Claire leans forward, wrapping her arms around my shoulders. "I was looking for you."

"I told you to stay with Ms. Bailey until I came to find you," I say, looking up at Laura with thankful eyes. "I have to meet with the other parents."

"I wanted to ride the bus with you."

I look behind her, watching as the clunky yellow buses maneuver through the narrow parking lot. It took two school vehicles to transport the kindergarten class of North Ridge Elementary to McCallister's Pumpkin Patch—Laura's class wasn't grouped with mine. When they pass, I see the line of parents waiting to get inside.

My attention is pulled away from Claire, back to my own class of fifteen students. They're standing in line, kicking at dirt and waiting for instruction. I'll have to get their attention before they catch sight of their parents, or, like Claire, they'll all take off in a variety of different directions.

"Ms. Howard's class, stay to the left," I tell the students, doing a quick count of heads. One through fifteen. They're all there. I turn back to Claire. "Stay with Ms. Bailey until I come to get you, okay?"

She nods without speaking, skipping back in the direction of her class. Laura smiles at me, shaking her head.

"She's more excited than I've seen her all year," she says. "All she talked about on the way over was exploring the pumpkin patch with Mommy."

"I'm excited, too," I say, looking at my clipboard. "Beats the classroom."

"And we have backup," she says, looking at the parents walking toward us. "Got to love a field trip."

Normally, going anywhere with over a dozen kinder-garteners is cause for me to double-up on my anxiety medica-tion, but this year is different, because Claire is here. She can't be in my homeroom—that would be too much of a distraction for both of us—but I can see her throughout the day ambling through the grade-level pod at school, playing in the playground at recess. And then there are days like today, when I get to feel a little less like a teacher and more like a parent.

I'm constantly being pulled between the two roles.

"Ms. Howard?" The first parent approaches me, holding a visitor sticker in her hand and a water bottle in the other.

"Aiden's mother, right?" I say, flicking through the papers on my clipboard. "Just sign here and he's yours the rest of the day. We'll have lunch at the pavilion around one o'clock, if you'd like to join us. The bus will head back to the school at two. Will he be riding with us or leaving with you?"

"He'll stay with me," she says, taking the pen and signing. "Do I need to check with you before we leave?"

"This is all I need," I say, nodding at the paperwork. I turn behind me, gesturing for Aiden to join us. "Just flag down me or one of the other teachers if you need anything."

I repeat the conversation another eleven times, making sure to answer each parent's questions. Some parents are veteran field trip chaperones, but others, especially if this is their first child, aren't quite sure what to expect. I always try to be consid-erate of them. Children are intimidating. With their little bodies and smiling faces, they hold so much power over us, and they don't even know it. Being responsible for the well-being of even one child is a large task. On field trip days, when there are so many children in one place, the stakes are even higher.

"Mommy?" Claire is pulling on the hem of my shirt again.

"Why aren't you with Ms. Bailey?"

She looks behind her and points. "She's right there."

"Yes, but you need to stay with her until we divide up the

rest of the students," I say. "I told you this before we left for school."

It was a hectic morning. My alarm went off late, which meant I was behind on making bagels and pouring coffee. I had to find our shirts, and make sure that our water bottles were packed. I styled Claire's hair into a ponytail because there was little time for anything else, and we bickered over the fact the hot-pink hair ribbon she wanted to wear clashed with her shirt. By the time we made it to the car, I was already irritated.

"I just want to stay with you," Claire says, and I wonder if she's being clingy now because she picked up on my frustration this morning.

"Just wait a little bit longer," I say, smiling, "and I'm yours the rest of the day."

This makes her happy, and she returns to Laura. As she does, I catch sight of the bright-pink ribbon tied around the top of her ponytail. She must have put it in when I wasn't looking.

Part of me wants to confront her about it, but I stop myself. She's only a little girl. What does she care if her outfit doesn't match? If it were up to her, she'd wear nothing but pink and purple every day. If David were here, he'd burst out laughing, take pride in our defiant daughter.

But David isn't here anymore. It's only me, and sometimes the weight of carrying everything on my own makes me want to break.

THREE

As more parent chaperones arrive to collect their children, the crowd thins, and I'm able to catch sight of my fellow teaching staff. We've agreed to meet under the pavilion to get our plans in order. Most students have parents attending the field trip, but those that don't will be split among the teachers. It's usually easier for the remaining students to stick with their homeroom, but occasionally we'll come up with a different plan depending on friend groups.

First to arrive at the pavilion is Mr. Shaver. Most people would look at Benjamin Shaver and assume he teaches older kids. With his stocky build and thick facial hair, he looks like he'd be better suited for running football plays than teaching the alphabet. However, I've worked with him for over a year now, and I've learned Ben is the stereotypical gentle giant. He grew up in foster care and credits his own kindergarten teacher with saving him from a dangerous home environment; it's the reason he's so at ease with the younger students, why he wants to make a difference.

"Hi, Ben," I say, instructing my students to sit next to his. "Off to a good start?"

"Yep. All my parents showed up on time. Looks like I'll have Sally Wren and Mary Wainwright with me today. How many are left in your homeroom?"

"Three. Jeff List, Calvin Barnes and Makayla Peters."

The three students I've just named have already made themselves at home beside their classmates, giggling and pawing at one another's jackets.

"I'm guessing your mini-me will stick with you," Ben says, as Laura brings her class over. Besides Claire, she has two other students left in her homeroom: Roger Smith and Katy Callaway.

"You can't beat this weather," Laura says, surveying the scene. "Looks like there are all sorts of activities."

Nothing is as idyllic as an October day at McCallister's Pumpkin Patch, although in East Tennessee, it's hard to tell what type of weather you might get. The mornings might feel like winter, which dips back into summer by the afternoon. Today, autumn has arrived in full. Clear blue skies, cool air, multicolored trees along the perimeter of the land, the foliage ranging from yellow and orange to purple and red.

There are plenty of attractions here, too. The obvious pumpkin fields, a petting zoo, two corn mazes and a playground. Normally, it would be a hassle chasing students from one place to the next, but I'm looking forward to it because Claire is here with me.

"I want to walk around with Makayla," Katy announces, playing with the bracelet around her wrist.

"Can Calvin be my buddy for the day?" Roger adds.

"Sit tight, everyone," I say. "We're still waiting on one class to join."

"I'm here!" Sarah Green shouts, waving her clipboard in the air. Two students are quick on her heels, kicking up dust.

Although I've worked with Laura the longest, Sarah is closest to my age. We've become best friends in the teaching pod, doing everything from organizing school events together to grouping up on the bus ride for today's field trip. She has short dark hair and equally dark eyes. No children of her own yet, but she's probably the closest thing Claire has to an aunt.

"Sorry, had a late parent," she says. "Have we already sorted chaperones?"

"We were waiting on you," Laura says. She looks at the students. "Although it seems some of them have already placed themselves in groups."

"Let's do a quick headcount," Ben says.

Between the four of us, there are ten kids without a parent chaperone. Nine, excluding Claire. Laura takes Makayla, Sally and Katy. The rowdiest students—Jeff, Calvin and Cole—are stuck with Ben. Sarah and I decide to walk around together, taking the remaining three with us.

"Lunch is at one o'clock, right?" Ben confirms.

"Yes. Anna and Jack are bringing lunch over from the cafeteria."

"Hopefully they'll stay until the end of the day," Ben says. "Give us some extra help."

"That's the plan," Laura says.

Anna and Jack are our kindergarten assistants. Truthfully, I'm not sure how any of us would make it through the day without them.

"Mommy, I have a question," Claire says, pulling on my shirt again.

"What is it, sweetheart?"

"I thought we were going to walk around. Just the two of us."

It's not really a question, but her intentions are clear. She wants to be like any other child on the trip. She wants to have her mother's attention all to herself. And I can't give her that.

"Look, we talked about this? Not everyone has a mommy or daddy who can leave work for a field trip." As soon as the words leave my lips, I curse myself. *Why did I say daddy?* I can't give her that either. I try to recover. "We're going to have fun today. We just have some of your classmates joining us. Okay?"

"Okay," she says, dissatisfied. "Can we go to the playground first thing?"

"Sure. Run on over."

She takes off, the other students in my homeroom running after her. Some of Sarah's students follow.

"I guess I'm sticking with you today," Sarah says, heading off after the children.

"We'll ride over to the pumpkin patch first thing," Ben says. "Beat the lines."

"Sounds like fun," Laura says, addressing her students, urging them to fall in line with Ben's group. She turns to me, her voice low and reassuring. "Don't worry about Claire. The two of you are going to have a great day together."

Just like that, responsibilities are sorted and settled. I walk in the direction of the playground, keeping an eye out for Claire and my other students, trying to leave behind the familiar feeling of not being able to give my daughter everything she needs.

FOUR

The key attraction at the pumpkin patch isn't the pumpkins. For a bunch of five- and six-year-olds, it's the ten-foot slide at the property's center, complete with matching swing sets on either side and an underground tunnel maze covered in powdery beige sand at the front. The slide itself is constructed from black plastic piping, in keeping with the rustic feel of the farm. The line to the top is already long, and those that don't fancy waiting are happy to chase after one another in the tunnels or grab an empty swing.

"Can I go on the slide?" Claire asks, squeezing my hand.

"Wait your turn," I say.

Claire and the other children in our group take off running. Sarah and I remain where we're standing, so we can keep a better view of everyone. None of the children can make it out of the area without passing by us.

"I often wonder, do you think parents actually enjoy these trips? Or is it as stressful for them as it is us?" Sarah asks. She pulls out her phone and starts texting.

"If I were here with *only* Claire, I think I'd enjoy myself, but I'm here as a teacher, too," I answer. "Having to wear both hats is daunting. I'm trying to make sure Claire gets all the attention she needs, while managing all my other responsibilities. Making sure Calvin has his inhaler and ensuring Jeff stays clear of the peanut stand..."

My dilemma is far bigger than this one day, I realize, after I've spoken the words aloud. Each day for the past two years has been a struggle, an indelicate balance between what I want to do and what needs to be done. Between what Claire needs and what I'm able to give her.

"At least the kids are having fun," Sarah says, pulling me back to the present. Cold air, loud children and the faint scent of soil. "I loved field trips when I was in school. Never even occurred to me how much work it is for the adults."

The next person to plop out of the slide tunnel is Claire. Her ponytail is whipped around her face, and she's smiling. I wave.

"You've done a good job with her, Emma," Sarah says, watching her with me. "Most people wouldn't have any idea what she's been through."

The smile on my face dips. Every moment, even happy ones like this, seem to delve back into sadness. I change the subject.

"So, what was your drama with the parent this morning?"

"Custody issue. Mom said it was her trip with Mavis, but Dad showed up. God forbid, the three of them just tough it out for one day."

"What ended up happening?"

"The dad stormed off, but not before causing a scene in the parking lot. I'm sure you'll hear about it."

"Did Mavis see?"

"I tried to keep her away from them until everything was sorted, but I'm afraid she heard more than I would have liked. I hate what these kids see sometimes. Maybe people are right when they say divorce is a fate worse than death."

There's a tense silence as Sarah's own words catch up to her.

"Oh my gosh, Emma. I'm so sorry. I shouldn't have said that."

"It's okay."

Sarah often puts her foot in her mouth, but she has good intentions. There was no malice behind her words.

"You know I didn't mean it—"

"It's fine, really. And you're right. It bothers me, too. Children are lucky to have both parents," I say. Poor Claire is only left with me. "It's a shame when the parents can't put aside their differences long enough to see that."

"It was an ugly scene. But Mavis seems to be enjoying herself now."

"Laura is having a similar issue," I say. "She was telling me about it earlier this week."

"From Katy Callaway's parents?"

"How did you know?"

"Katy's father works with my sister. From what she says, their divorce is ugly. The mother is going for full custody."

"That's what Laura said. The mother has pulled her in to meetings. She's even trying to get her to write out a deposition, something that will help her when she takes her case to court."

"From what my sister says, the father seems like a stand-up guy. I'm not sure what caused the divorce. But I guess you never really know how a person acts behind closed doors."

"The mother is nice, too. We went to school together, ages ago. I just hope whatever plan they make is what's best for Katy, and not themselves."

"Hey! One at a time!" Sarah yells at a trio of students messing around at the swing set. She's so loud, I jump. "Did I scare you?"

"Don't worry about me. Let's just get these kids home safely."

"No broken bones would be a win for me." She pulls her phone out again and starts pounding on the screen.

"Everything okay?" I ask Sarah. "You've barely put that thing away since we got here."

But it's not just the constant screen time. She seems distracted. Sarah, Laura and I have worked together the longest —the Three Amigas, we call ourselves. Having spent so many countless hours on the job with the same people, it's easy to tell when someone is acting off.

"It's nothing," she says, but her words ring false, and she knows it. She sighs and slides her phone inside her jacket. "Darren and I are having problems again."

I could have guessed. Even though they live together and have dated for ages, there always seems to be drama.

"What is it this time?"

"Remember that job he started last month?"

"Yes. Working with his brother, right?" My tone is positive, recalling how excited Sarah was when she told me about it. A *real* job. One that included benefits and security.

"Well, he already quit. Said his brother accused him of fudging the numbers on the books, so he caused a scene and left." She crosses her arms over her chest, as though she's trying hard not to unleash her full aggravation. "You can't just up and quit the moment you disagree with someone. Life doesn't work that way. Hell, if we quit every time our job got stressful, there'd be no teachers left!"

I choose my words carefully. Although Darren has never impressed me, I know how quickly this fight could blow over like all the others. As frustrated as Sarah is with him, she's never been upset enough to actually leave.

"What did he say when you told him he can't act that way?"

"That this is *his* life, and he has to do what makes *him* happy," she says, in a mocking voice. "I mean what about *our* life? You know, my sister is getting married this winter. Of course, I'm happy for her, but do you know how long she's known the guy? Six months! Darren and I have been together for six *years*, and he still isn't ready to commit to me. Or a job. Or anything, it seems."

Darren is unconventional, and the one time she brought up marriage to him, he got antsy, so she never approached the subject again. That was three years ago. Sarah wants a husband and a wedding and kids, and if she's too afraid to be honest about those needs, I worry she's wasting time with the wrong person. Even my brother-in-law, the eternal bachelor, eventually settled down and married, but sometimes I worry Darren isn't cut from the same cloth. If I was a better friend, maybe I'd have the nerve to tell her that.

"You know, sometimes people just want different things. It's better that you're both honest about what you want."

"The thing is, I *was* honest. I told him last night I can't keep putting my life on pause while he figures out what he wants to do with his."

I'm impressed. Sarah hasn't always been this assertive. When she first started working at North Ridge Elementary, she was fresh out of college, her resumé blank, but her head full of Pinterest-worthy ideas for how to make the classroom, and the world, a better place. She was hit with a steep learning curve, the harsh realities of teaching in a public school: low budgets, countless observations, testing data and achievement benchmarks for students just learning to write their own names.

I can still remember finding her behind her desk one day after school, sobbing into the sleeves of her cardigan. We walked outside, and I watched as she smoked cigarette after cigarette, listened as she voiced all her frustrations about the job. Only a few weeks in, and she was ready to quit. She hadn't realized that working with children could be so much *work*.

From then on, Laura and I rallied around her, as did our other co-teachers at the time, assured her that we had all experienced the same growing pains and we'd help her make it to the other side. Over the years, in addition to gaining a close friend, I've witnessed Sarah become a stronger person, a more confident teacher. Now, she's all the things she once aspired to be in the classroom, energetic and compassionate. But when it comes to her relationship with Darren, I catch glimpses of the unsure girl she was before.

"And?" I ask, focusing back on the present crisis.

"It turned into an ugly fight." When she looks away, I wonder if it's because she's trying not to cry. "He says I'm trying to *control* him, and I swear that's not what I'm trying to do. I believe we could be so happy together, if he'd just bend a little. But I can't keep carrying us both. Financially. Emotionally. It's wearing me down."

"I'm sorry," I say, placing a gentle hand on her arm. It's possible these are the most honest words she's ever shared. "You have a good head on your shoulders. It sounds like you're starting to lead with that, and not just your heart. Everything will work out the way it should."

"I don't know if it will this time. How long can you sit around waiting for something you want? Eventually, you have to do something about it." She shakes her head. "Anyway, the whole situation has me distracted. I just need the weekend to process everything. I'll be a new Sarah come Monday."

"As long as you're still the Sarah I love," I say, squeezing her hand.

I hate that I can't offer more guidance, especially since she's been such a huge support system for me in the past two years. Truth is, I know very little about relationships and love. I'd had my share of breakups and heartbreaks when I was younger, but once I met David, all that faded away. Our relationship was easy, from our first date to our engagement to the day we got married. There were mornings I'd literally pinch myself, thinking I didn't deserve the perfect life we'd created together.

Turns out I was right: I didn't deserve it.

And it's a happiness I fear I'll never be able to recapture.

FIVE

The left field of the pumpkin patch has an old barn that has been converted into a petting zoo, another highlight for the students. There are miniature horses, two spotted cows, and curious hens pecking at the hard soil. Sheep with dingy white wool lounge in the far corner of the stalls, their neighbors, the energetic goats, sprinting nearby. Two llamas wander by the front gate, eyeing each visitor skeptically.

By the entrance of the barn is a small shed where students can collect small pellets of food in ice-cream cones to feed the animals. We've gathered our group, and are headed in that direction, when my phone pings.

"It's Anna," I tell Sarah, looking at the text. "She and Jack are here with the food."

"Isn't it a little early?"

My watch says it's half past eleven. Two full hours have already passed in a blink, and we've yet to visit even half of the attractions.

"It will take a while to get everything unloaded and set up. Nothing worse than waiting on hungry students. And parents."

"You go help them," Sarah says. "I can take this group

through the barn. By the time we finish, it will be almost time to eat."

"Sounds good."

"Mommy, I wanted to feed the animals with you," Claire says. She's holding her ice-cream cone with two tight hands, but bits of food still fall to the ground.

"I'll only be a minute. Maybe you and I can walk back over, before the bus leaves?"

She doesn't seem satisfied, but she nods.

I march in the direction of the pavilion. Above, the skies are a pearly gray, the wind growing just a bit colder. Pockets of sunshine break through the clouds, and only in those spots do I feel any warmth.

David and I used to love spending time outdoors during the fall, and an afternoon at McCallister's Pumpkin Patch was a yearly tradition. There were many visits when it was just the two of us. We'd load up a basket with sandwiches and snacks, hide a bottle of wine beneath gingham napkins. David, an aspiring musician, would carry his guitar across his back in its case.

We'd eventually find a quiet spot where the two of us could have lunch and drink. After our meal, once the bottle of wine was close to empty, he'd pull out his guitar and begin playing, sometimes songs he'd written, but mostly just ones he knew I liked. It was a peaceful time, before the seasons of our lives changed, and we became professionals and parents.

After Claire was born, David and I returned. Some of my favorite family photos were taken in the fields to my right, where the bright orange pumpkins shine bright against the forest.

This is the first time we've been back since David died.

I wonder if Claire has glimpses of memory about this place. Or her father. Probably not, and I'm always too afraid to ask. As Sarah and Laura and everyone else always tells me, Claire is well-adjusted, but I'm too afraid to bring up her father when she seems so happy.

"Emma! Over here."

On the opposite side of the pavilion, I spy Anna Russo and Jack Fox. Both are wearing the same burnt-orange shirt as everyone else. Their hands are full, stacked high with boxes that rest just below their chins.

"I'm coming to help," I shout. "You don't have to carry so many at once."

"There are plenty more," Jack says. "You can help with the next load."

Jack is in his late twenties, slim and strong, with blond hair brushed to the side. He started working at the school last year and is halfway through earning his own teaching degree. He attends night classes at the local community college, often leaning on the rest of the team to help him edit and revise his various assignments.

Anna walks close behind him, her waist-length brown hair plaited and swinging with each step. She's the newest member of our group. She earned her degree last spring but finding a K-2 opening in the area has been difficult. Even though there has been a nationwide teacher shortage in the wake of the pandemic, most turnover tends to happen in older grade levels. They're both hoping to pad their resumés enough so that when there is an opening, they're the first ones to be considered.

We'll take help in any form we can get it; our grade level would feel lost without the extra set of hands. As assistants, they work with all the students and teachers, providing one-on-one readings and an extra pair of eyes, when needed.

My boots crunch against the gravel as I follow them out to the car lot, which is now so full with guest vehicles I'm surprised they were able to find a place to park. We stop in front of Anna's Nissan.

"There's one more load in the back," she says. "The three of us should be able to carry them over."

"How are the kids enjoying the field trip?" Jack asks.

"Having a blast, so far," I say. "Sarah has my group over at the petting zoo."

"I forgot Claire is with you today," Anna says. "Head back. You should spend the day with her."

"I don't mind. It's a lot of work setting up food for sixty people."

"We've got this, really," Jack says. "Everything will be ready by the time you get back."

"If you're sure."

They both wave me along, before unloading more Styrofoam containers. As I look back, I see them whispering, then Anna rears back with a full-body guffaw. Jack is leaned over, trying to steady his grip on the containers as he joins her laughter. Watching them together makes me smile. Before they came along, our assistants were either retired teachers looking to supplement their pensions or stay-at-home parents looking for an excuse to be closer to their kids during the day. Having two college kids in the mix has added some lightness to the group, something else I'll take in whatever form I can get it.

It's also refreshing knowing there are still people who genuinely want to enter the field, despite its shortcomings and challenges. Anna and Jack, as well as the rest of our team, all aim to make a difference in our students' lives. That's how I felt when I started teaching, although my priorities have shifted. I'm still grateful to come to work every day, but it's always in the back of my mind that I no longer have this job because I want it —I need it. Since David's death, my measly state salary is the only income I have.

As I approach the barn, I take in the long tubular slide. It must be ten feet high. Although it's enclosed, I still think of the potential danger. The opening at the entrance is just wide enough that a small child could slip through, landing hard on the straw-covered ground beneath my feet. We always instruct the children to be careful, but when there are so many little ones fighting for a turn, accidents can happen.

"Is someone inside the barn monitoring the kids?" I say, afraid to take my eyes away from the entrance to the slide.

"Ben is up there," Sarah says. "It's hard to see, but he said he'd man the line."

I feel better knowing there is an adult nearby.

A scream echoes. The sound grows louder, the voice jostling as it comes closer. From the exit of the slide pops out a pair of legs, then a torso, then finally a face, with a bright-pink ribbon tied into her hair. It's Claire. She's smiling, still laughing from her trip down the slide.

"Mommy!" she says, when she sees me, and instead of running back to the barn for a second turn, as all the other children do, she comes to me. "You're back."

"Told you I'd only be a minute."

"Did you see me go down the slide?"

"I got here just in time."

"Can I go again?"

"Have at it," I say.

She gives me a hug before rushing off.

"Time for a quick headcount," Sarah says, walking in the direction of the barn.

I'm left alone with the other parent chaperones, smiling as we watch the children race to the top of the slide platform, trying not to think about how dangerous one little misstep could be.

SIX

After a bit of nagging, we're able to gather all the children and start our trek away from the animal barn.

"You think we have time to ride over to the pumpkin field before lunch?" Sarah asks. She's looking at her phone again, even though she promised to stop thinking about Darren.

"We have forty-five minutes before we're supposed to meet at the pavilion," I say, checking my watch. "How long does the ride take?"

"Half an hour. Or less." She shrugs. "Looks like the trailer is pulling up now. We'll be back in time."

Claire and our other three students wander in front of us. We've already tackled the playground, the petting zoo and the Barn Slide of Death. If we ride over to the patch now, we won't have much to fit in after lunch.

"Let's hop on," I say.

We're helping the students onto the wagon, one-by-one, when Mary slips. She lands on the ground and lets out a cry, her small hands covering her knee.

"Are you okay?" Sarah reaches her before I can.

"It hurts."

I look over Sarah's shoulder. When Mary pulls back her hands, there's a small abrasion on her knee.

"Oh no," Sarah says. "There's a little bit of blood. We'll need to get that cleaned up."

"I'm sure they have a first-aid kit available at the ticket stand."

Sarah looks back at the trailer, which is filling up with students and parents. "I don't want to leave you alone with all the kids."

"It's fine, really."

Just then, Anna wanders over from the pavilion. Her head turns in the direction of Mary's cries. "What's happened here?"

"Just a little fall," I say, helping Mary to her feet. "We were getting ready to take the rest of the kids on the pumpkin patch ride."

"I'm heading back to search for a first-aid kit," Sarah says. She turns to Anna. "Care to ride with Emma over to the pumpkin fields?"

"Sure." As usual, Anna doesn't hesitate to help.

"Thanks." Sarah gathers Mary in her arms. "We'll be all better in no time. See you at the pavilion?"

"Sounds good." I count the remaining children to make sure they're all on board, scooting over to make room for Anna beside me. "Let's take off."

The ride across the street to the pumpkin patch is bumpy, but the kids love it, giggling and swaying at every turn. Once the wagon stops, we've no sooner helped everyone off before Claire is tugging at my shirt.

"Will you help me pick my pumpkin?" she asks.

"Sure. Maybe Roger can come with us. He'll probably need help carrying."

She doesn't say anything, but the look on her face is enough.

"You two go ahead," Anna says, resting her hands on Roger's shoulders. "I can handle these guys."

"Are you sure?"

"We have only a few minutes before we go back to the chaos," she says. "Enjoy it."

We're only a stone's throw away from the other side of the property, but it feels like an entirely different location. Gone are the man-made entertainment structures and loud voices and running children. The pumpkin field is as peaceful as it is picturesque. Some of the parents that joined us on the ride are posing their children for pictures.

"Want to take a selfie?" I ask.

Claire nods and prepares a pose. She loves taking pictures. At night, when she's still restless, we'll sometimes lie in bed and play around with the different filters on my phone, making funny faces. Most nights, she falls asleep in my room. I quit moving her about six months ago. I so miss the feeling of having another person beside me.

I snap the picture and show her the screen. We both approve.

"Which way do we go?" Claire asks me.

"You lead the way."

The ground is uneven, so we're mindful of every move, stepping over writhing vines and divots in the soil. Most of the pumpkins beside the road are small, but Claire wants to venture further into the field in search of a bigger one.

"Let's not go too far," I tell her. "We don't want the others waiting on us."

"I'm looking for the right one," she says, passing three oblong pumpkins that look the exact same.

"Okay, Charlie Brown," I say, trudging behind her.

"Here." She places her hand on a large, round pumpkin. "What do you think of this one?"

"I think it's perfect." And no different than the other dozen we passed to get here, but it makes me happy that she picked it. "Now find a good one for me."

She's not as selective when it comes to mine but chooses one around the same size.

"They'll match," she says.

Because they're so big, I'm left carrying both the short distance it takes to reach the truck. Once we arrive, I see that Anna and her group are already seated while the group waits for a few more people to return.

"Looks like you found some good ones," Anna says, sliding down the wooden bench to make more room.

"I like yours, too," I tell the other students. Claire sits beside them, showing off her own pumpkin.

The ride back to the main grounds seems to take longer, but that's only because my stomach is beginning to growl.

"I'm starving," I say. "It must be all this walking around."

"Jack should have everything set up by the time we get back."

"Speaking of Jack, how is it going with the two of you?"

Her cheeks turn red. "Is it that obvious?"

"I pick up on these things. Especially when we all work so closely together."

"We've been seeing each other a couple of weeks. I've been trying to keep it under wraps."

"He's a catch. We all know the other moms swoon over him."

She laughs. "Please. Don't embarrass me."

"It's a compliment. You two make a cute couple."

"It's still new, but I think there's potential," she says. "Clearly, we both love kids. We have the same interests outside of work, too, even though he's busy during the week with his night classes."

"It's good that your goals line up."

I think about Sarah and her issues with Darren. That's what she needs. Someone who wants the same things out of life that she does.

"We spend most of our time together on the weekends," she says. "Last Saturday, we went hiking near the Bluffs. That's one of our favorite spots in town. Have you ever been?"

Even though I grew up in the area, I was never big about the outdoors until I met David. He and his brother spent most of their time outside. Camping. Hunting. Fishing. For our first anniversary, David set up a small campsite at the Bluffs. I was reluctant to spend the night at first, but once we were there, alone in the quiet night, staring up at a blanket of stars, I felt at home. Looking back, I think that's the night I realized I could love this man forever.

"It's years since I've been," I say. "It's a beautiful place. I'm happy for you two."

Anna looks at the children, who are busy in their own conversations, before asking her next question. "What about you? Are you seeing anyone?"

"No. I'm not there yet."

Everyone is aware of my situation, even though Ben, Jack and Anna didn't join the team until after David died. We've all become so close, I sometimes forget they weren't around when it happened, especially since they've all witnessed my grief in one way or another.

The most obvious moment that comes to mind is the one-year anniversary of David's death. In the days leading up to it, Sarah and Laura suggested I stay home, take some time for myself, but I was stubborn, determined to prove that I was stronger than they gave me credit for. So, I went to work, treated it like it was any other day.

It was a mistake.

I made it through the morning without incident. Took Claire to daycare. Settled into my own classroom. My students and I went over our letter for the week, read our class story, completed an art project. The morning was so busy, I rarely had time to think about the significance of the day itself. It wasn't until I was alone in my classroom, my students away at lunch, that it hit me.

One entire year without David. An entire round of holidays I had to reinvent and suffer through. Countless nights of listening to Claire cry, trying to comfort her, knowing nothing I said would ever fully make her pain go away.

Anna found me first. She had only been working at North Ridge for a couple of weeks at the time. I'm certain she knew about David, but she wasn't ready to handle my meltdown. Jack stood in the doorway, keeping a nervous eye on me, as she ran to grab the other teachers.

"Emma, tell us what's going on," Laura said when she entered the room, immediately rushing to me and putting her arms around me.

"It's been a whole year without him," I let out between breaths. "It's like I didn't fully realize that until this moment."

Sarah was standing on the other side of me, her arm wrapped around my shoulders. "You've been so strong," she said. "I don't know how you've done it. I wouldn't be able to hold it together like you have."

"I'm not holding it together! I'm falling apart."

"It's okay to fall apart," Jack said, coming into the room. "Sometimes that's the only way to get better."

"But it's not just me I'm worried about. Claire. I need to stay strong for her, and I can't."

"You're an excellent mother," Laura said.

"Claire is lucky to have you," Sarah added.

"Maybe what you really need is some time," Ben added, finally speaking up. "Go home for the rest of the day. Take some time to yourself. We can split up your class."

"No," I said, wiping my tears. "I can't do that."

"Yes, you can," Ben insisted. "You need a break."

"I can pick up Claire from daycare," Sarah said. "We'll grab dinner and head to your house after school."

"It's okay to ask for help, Emma," Anna said.

"We *want* to help you," Ben added.

And then there they were, all five of them, huddled around me, each with their different personalities and experiences, but united in their mission: to let me know I would be okay. It's a moment I'll never forget, a rare moment of grace in a year that was otherwise dominated by darkness.

"People must be getting hungry," Anna says, pulling me out of my memories and back to the present. As the trailer gets closer to the main grounds, we can see there's already a line of parents waiting to get food.

"Thanks for riding over with me," I tell Anna, even though, in my mind, I'm thankful for her help with everything, not just today.

"No problem. It takes a village, right?"

We help the students off the trailer, careful not to have any more injuries. We make our way to the pavilion and find Jack already standing behind a picnic table, serving lunch to the people in line.

Anna turns to me. "Don't tell the other teachers, okay?"

"My lips are sealed." I smile. "Run on ahead. I'm going to wait for Sarah."

Anna joins Jack at the picnic table, helping him hand out the lunch boxes. Even from this distance, I can see the glow on both their faces, that subtle light that develops at the start of something new. It's the same light I felt that night at the Bluffs, all those years ago.

From across the field, Sarah comes marching into the frame, the first-aid kit tucked under her arm. She's tapping at her phone again. Likely arguing with Darren. It's unnerving seeing her like this. Aged and tired. As Sarah struggles to find the best way to end a relationship, Anna is trying to start a new one.

Then there's me. I've already loved and lost. And I'm not sure what direction my heart will go in next.

SEVEN

Sarah, Jack and I stand behind the picnic table situated at the front of the pavilion, disposable aprons wrapped around our waists. Anna is at the entrance, telling parents and students to see us if they'd like a complimentary lunch. I suspect most parents will leave the field trip early enough to grab food at one of the restaurants nearby, but it appears there are plenty of hungry mouths left to feed. The line grows long.

"What's on the menu?" Sarah asks.

"Hot dogs. Chips. And choice of drink," Jack answers, handing off another Styrofoam container to one of the bundled-up moms. "I'm told the apple juice pairs best with the entrée."

The mom laughs, as does the one behind her. It's not that funny a joke, really. But when it's delivered by someone as young and charming as Jack, it gets a bigger reaction. It's not often you find a man that's handsome, kind, and patient with children. Add the fact that he's single, and Jack Fox is the ulti-mate catch. From the way Anna was talking about him earlier, I believe she knows how lucky she is.

"No! Don't!"

A woman's voice rings out from the back of the pavilion.

Seconds later, there's the sound of something falling, followed by several gasps. We all turn in that direction.

"It's okay," a mother shouts. "We've had a spill."

"I'm on it," Jack says, rushing over with a roll of paper towels.

"If that's the worst thing that happens all day, I'd say we're good," Sarah says. "By the way, when he gets back, feel free to take off. I was hoping for some one-on-one time with him."

I laugh. "Are you serious? Jack?"

"Why not? He's single. I'm... kinda single."

"I thought you and Darren were arguing. I didn't think this was an actual breakup?"

"I don't know what it is, but I know I'm tired. If Darren isn't ready to commit, I'm not sticking around."

"And you think starting something up with a guy from work is a good idea? Not to mention he's almost ten years younger than us."

"It's not a bad idea. Is it? Maybe I need someone young and fun in my life."

Across the way, the mess is already cleaned up and the soiled napkins trashed. Jack stands at the front with Anna. The two of them are smiling. Sarah follows my stare. It only takes her a few seconds to see what I see.

"Wait. Are the two of them..." She looks back at me, her jaw lowering.

I've just promised Anna not to mention her relationship, but the last thing our team needs is a love triangle messing with the group dynamics. I shrug my shoulders, letting Sarah work it out for herself.

She drops her hands. "Just my luck. Someone who wants the life I'm after, and he's already snatched up. As if I could compete with a woman in her twenties."

"I think it's still the early stages," I say. "Don't worry. Whether it's Jack or Darren, the right guy will come around."

My eyes wander back to the new couple. Seeing them together, a knowing smile spreads across my face. Then a sourer feeling takes over, when I realize my chance at having that sensation is gone forever.

David is never coming back.

At least Sarah has the possibility of thinking love is just around the corner. The person I'm meant to be with is gone, buried in the ground at North Ridge Cemetery.

David's funeral was small and private, only immediate family invited. His older brother, Steven, was there, red-eyed and half drunk. Steven was never a big drinker, but it seemed the only way he could make it through the day. We avoided each other as much as possible, which wasn't an easy task considering how few people were in attendance. Claire spent most of the day with David's great-aunt Mildred, busying herself with coloring books and sticker sheets, anything to keep her mind away from the permanence of her father's death.

The funeral was short, followed by an even shorter grave-side service. After the minister had delivered his final prayers, the other mourners trekked back to their cars. Steven stumbled off, saying he'd meet us back at the house, when he was really heading to the nearest bar. Mildred kept Claire with her, giving me a few minutes alone.

I stood by David's grave, thinking of all my memories. It seemed like there were so many, and yet they weren't enough. My mind revisited our last conversation, my chest feeling as though it was clenching shut, when I felt a hand on my shoulder.

"Are you okay?" It was Sarah.

Standing beside her, was Laura. "I hope it's okay that we came."

They'd come without being asked. They came because they knew I needed them.

I'm not sure how long we stayed by David's grave that afternoon, but Laura and Sarah refused to let me be alone. The Three Amigas, still standing by each other's sides on the saddest of days.

The sounds of squealing children pull me back to the present.

"Finally, we made it."

Ben comes behind the table, slinging his backpack on the ground. He sounds agitated.

"Everything okay?"

"I couldn't get Jeff and Calvin to leave the animal barn. I had to climb to the top of that godforsaken slide three different times to bring them down." He huffs. "Look, I know they're only kindergartners, but I think we should leave the rowdy students behind. For the sake of everyone else."

Ben's dry tone makes it hard to tell whether he's being serious, but I've worked alongside him long enough to know this is only his sense of humor.

"Let's give them lunch," I say. "Everyone is much more cooperative on a full stomach."

"Any sign of Laura?" Sarah asks.

"I saw her near the animal barn, but I was distracted with my own bunch," Ben says.

"What about the parents?" I ask.

"The grounds looked empty. I'd say the ones still here are eating with us, and the others have left."

"All right," I say, taking off my apron. "If we're only waiting on one more group, I'm going to go ahead and eat. I promised Claire I'd sit with her."

"Yes, go. Enjoy yourself," Sarah says.

Claire and her friends are sitting at the picnic table closest to us; it's easier to keep an eye on them that way. When she sees me walking over with my lunch container, she begins wiggling in her seat.

"Are you having fun?"

"Yep." She nods, her ponytail bouncing with each dip of her head. "Mommy, when can we turn my pumpkin into a jack-o'-lantern?"

"Let's see," I say. "Halloween is one week away. How about we carve them tonight?"

"Really?"

"We can pick up a kit on the way home. Sounds like a great way to spend a Friday night."

Claire zips her arm through the air. "Yes!"

I look back at the food table. Ben and Sarah are sitting on a bench nearby, eating their own lunches. Behind them, I see Laura and her group finally making their way to the pavilion. The students skip ahead of her. It's not until she's closer, her eyes scanning the area, that I take in the look on Laura's face.

She's clearly agitated. And not angry, in the way Ben was only moments ago. It goes deeper than that. She appears worried, frightened.

I stand, making my way to her, but even when I reach her, it's like she's staring right through me.

"Is everything okay?"

Her throat trembles, tears filling her eyes. Laura is never distracted or distraught, not on the job. Something terrible must have happened.

"We were at the animal barn," she says, "then we went back to the playground. They were all right there..." Her words trail away.

"Laura." I put my hands on her shoulders, trying to steady her. "What's going on?"

"I... I was gathering up all the kids, but I couldn't find Katy Callaway. Is she here?"

My head spins round in the direction of the picnic chairs, counting each head, scanning each face. I haven't seen her since we last left Laura's group, and don't see her now.

"No. I don't think so. How long has it been since you last saw her?"

"One minute she was with the group, then she was gone. We retraced our steps before making our way over here. I've been looking for... fifteen minutes?" She pauses for a breath. "My God, Emma, I've lost a student."

EIGHT

She's gone.

It's every teacher's worst fear. Losing sight of a student, even for a moment.

It happens, of course. When we're lining up for a restroom break, marching to the cafeteria, or preparing for class dismissal. You count each person, and when you're one short, it's like your heart seizes, refusing to beat.

Then you see a head poking out from behind the door, or a straggler leaning against the wall. You count a second time and breathe a sigh of relief when you realize you've only miscalculated.

Everyone is accounted for. Everyone is fine. Everyone is safe.

Life continues.

But if the seconds stretch together, amount to a full minute, let alone fifteen, a tense fear takes hold. I can feel that fear now, clawing at my chest. I can see that fear painted in the expression on Laura's face.

"Everything okay?"

It's Ben. Sarah stands beside him. Even from across the

pavilion, their teacher senses have kicked in. They know some-thing is wrong.

Laura looks ahead, too rattled to speak.

"It's Katy Callaway," I say. "We can't find her."

Just as I did, Sarah and Ben raise their chins, scanning each picnic table.

"Where did you last see her?" Sarah asks Laura.

"The animal barn," Laura stammers. "She was right there with everyone else. Then she was just... gone."

"I'm sure she's just taken off somewhere," Sarah says, her voice calm. "Or she might have wandered off and joined one of the other groups without you noticing."

"All the groups are here," Ben says under his breath, a little more edge to his voice.

"Right." It's clear Sarah is struggling to find the right words to de-escalate the situation. "These things happen. She's around here somewhere."

"This has never happened to me before," Laura says, her eyes scanning the crowd in front of us, hopeful Katy will appear. "What if she's lost and scared? What if she's hurt?"

I walk Laura back to one of the picnic tables and force her to sit. By this point, Anna and Jack have sensed the tension, and have come closer. They stand on the periphery, trying to hear what is being said without interfering.

"You stay here," I tell Laura. "When you've calmed down, you can start asking around the pavilion. See if anyone has seen her."

"We don't want to start a panic," Ben says, a warning.

"No, but someone might remember seeing her," I say. "I'll head back to the animal barn, see if she's still there."

"I'll come with you," Ben says.

"What's wrong?" Jack says, finally finding the courage to ask.

I keep my voice low, so the parents won't hear. "Katy Callaway is missing."

Jack and Anna share a look, a strange stillness to each of their faces. They don't cover situations like this in education textbooks. Our courses were designed to prevent a situation like this from happening, but offer little help when a true problem presents itself.

"When's the last time anyone saw her?" Anna asks, stepping forward. There's a grave tone in her voice—in everyone's voice—that sends a chill up my spine.

"It's been fifteen minutes. Probably closer to twenty now." I turn, looking in the direction of the animal barn. "Ben and I are going to search where she was last seen."

"I'll stay here with Laura," Sarah volunteers, her eyes bouncing nervously between us.

"We can inform the property staff. Maybe they'll help us look," Jack says, nodding toward Anna. "See if she's wandered off somewhere else on the grounds."

"That's good," I say. The more people we have looking, the faster we will find her.

"We all have cell phones, right?" Anna asks.

Everyone's hands go straight to their devices. "If anyone finds her, send a message out to the others," I say. "We'll meet back here in twenty minutes."

Agreed on the plan, we all start off in our respective directions.

"Mommy!" Claire calls when she sees me walking away. In the panic of the last few minutes, I'd forgotten she was here.

"I have to check on something," I say to her, trying to keep my voice level. "Stay here with the others, and we'll head back to the playground soon."

She falls into conversation with the student behind her, but I have a sinking feeling in my stomach. We're all hoping this is a straightforward scenario, a child who has wandered off, but what if it's more serious? What if she's injured herself on one of the countless hazards on the property? With no adult watching her, there's no telling what she could have gotten into. This might not be resolved in the next twenty minutes.

"Go on, I've got the kids," Sarah tells me. "Ben is taking off without you."

I see him marching up the hill. Before I chase after him, I give Sarah one more order.

"Don't let any of the parents leave the pavilion," I say. "Not until we find Katy."

NINE

I'm out of breath by the time I catch up with Ben, and I'm not sure if it's because of the light jog, or if it's from the adrenaline.

"The barn is divided into a half-dozen rooms," he says. "It's not surprising that she'd get confused. I'm betting she's there."

His words come out assured, but there is an edge to his voice, like he's afraid we won't find her.

After a year of working with Ben, I'm aware of his tendency to wear his emotions on his sleeve. You can see his aggravation from across the playground as easily as you can hear his hearty chuckle from across the hall. I've only seen him lose his temper once. There was a substitute who was getting frustrated with one of the children. She grabbed the student's arm so hard it left a mark. Even though it wasn't Ben's student—the woman was actually watching over Sarah's kids—he witnessed the incident and went berserk. He yelled at the substitute in front of teachers and students alike, then marched the woman to the front office and demanded she be barred from the sub list.

We all understood his outrage, but I'd be lying if I said his anger didn't startle me, especially in a professional setting. The substitute tried to cause trouble for Ben, saying he'd been the one to put his hands on the student, but we all rallied around him. He was acting in the best interest of the children. That's all we ever try to do.

We reach the barn, which is empty, except for the livestock filling the stalls. A muddied walkway covered in trampled straw leads us from one end of the barn to the next, and there are waist-high gates keeping the animals enclosed.

The smell of manure hijacks my senses. I lift the collar of my shirt and cover the bottom half of my face. To my left, a miniature horse rests on a mound of hay. Across from it, a beige llama stands near the gate, ready to feed. There are goats and chickens and pigs, but no sign of Katy. I take out my phone, shining it into each stall.

"What are you doing?" Ben asks.

"It's dark in the back. I'm making sure Katy didn't get the bright idea to climb in and join the animals."

"I guess it's not completely beyond reason. I had to tell Jeff ten times to get off the gates."

He walks around to the other side of the barn, checking all the animal stalls. A few minutes pass before we meet again.

"She's not on the other side. I've looked everywhere." Ben looks up at the low-rise ceiling above our heads. "Let's check the second floor. See if she decided to ride the slide and never came down."

It's common for children to get scared once they see just how high the slide is. Maybe Katy got scared to ride it down but was too afraid to come back down the stairs. As the barn became quieter, and she realized she was alone, she might have decided to stay there.

"Watch your step," Ben says.

I follow him up the narrow staircase that leads to the second floor, holding the wood railing to keep myself balanced. A half hour ago, there were dozens of kids climbing these steps. Their presence breathed a chaotic energy into the place.

When it's only the two of us, the place feels barren and dangerous.

We reach the loft, which is covered with more hay and giant tubs filled with corn kernels. The kids play in them, like they would in a sandbox or a ball pit. There are even some shovels and toys strewn about.

"Katy!" Ben cups his hands around his mouth as he calls her name. "Katy, are you up here?"

There's another staircase that leads to the entrance of the slide. I can see clearly from where I stand, but I climb the steps anyway, looking to see if Katy has ducked inside the tunnel. Maybe she's hiding from us, thinking this is a game.

I dip my head inside the black tunnel and look down. I see a clear view of the ground below, nothing else.

"She's not up here," Ben yells. "I'm going back down. I'm going to check the stalls one more time."

I carefully climb down, each creak of the wood heightening my nerves. I hadn't considered how dangerous this place really is. How many places there are to get lost or hurt. I make it to the main level just as Ben is coming around the corner.

"She's not here." He sounds irritated now. "Have you heard from the others?"

The words no sooner leave his lips than both of our phones vibrate. It's a group message from Anna.

Told staff. No one has seen her.

A few seconds later, Sarah chimes in.

She's not at the pavilion.

"Christ, they haven't found her," Ben says aloud. "What was Laura thinking?"

"Hey, this isn't Laura's fault. It could have happened to any of us."

The human reaction is to place blame somewhere, especially when there isn't an easy scapegoat in sight.

"I know." He sounds guilty for lashing out. "But she should have told us as soon as she knew something was wrong."

"She did. I could tell just by looking at her something had happened."

Ben exhales, pressing his lips together, debating whether he should say anything. "I think Katy has been missing for longer than Laura is saying."

"What would make you think that?"

"You know my group was here, too. I was busy trying to get my students together for lunch. But I saw Laura running around the barn, like she was looking for someone."

"She was probably doing the same thing you were," I say. "Getting the group together."

"But she looked worried. As worried as she did at the pavilion. I should have said something to her, but I didn't."

"When was this?"

"A good twenty minutes before she arrived for lunch. Which means Katy would have been missing longer than she said."

"Closer to forty-five minutes." I try to calculate the time in my head. "Maybe even an hour."

"Knowing Laura, she didn't think much of it. Then, so much time passed, she was probably scared to say anything."

"If Katy has been gone that long, she could be anywhere."

"We need to get back to the others," Ben says. "We have a lot more land to cover, and we need to do it fast."

"I'm going to call the police."

"It can't be that serious, can it? I mean, there's enough adults that we can split up and find her ourselves."

"I don't want to take any chances. If a child has been

missing that long, it's more serious than just losing sight of someone."

"What's the school's protocol? Should I call back to the office and find out?"

"You call the school. I'll call the cops."

"You know once you call 911 this will turn into a big situation."

For some reason, my mind returns to the drama with the substitute. It was a worrisome situation for Ben, even though he was doing what was right for the child. Could he be wanting to hold off from calling the police because he doesn't want another negative incident on his record?

Or perhaps Ben is only being practical. He's thinking about the panic that could break out. How a situation like this could change school policy, even lead to lawsuits. We're responsible for keeping these children safe, and if something bad were to happen to a student under our care, all of us could face the brunt of it.

Then I remember Katy might have been missing for close to an hour.

"We don't have a choice," I say, reaching for my phone. "I'm calling it in."

TEN

When we arrive at the pavilion, it's clear word has started to spread.

"Ms. Howard," says a woman. I recognize her as one of the people I gave directions to this morning. "Can you tell me what's going on? Some of the other parents are saying a child is missing."

I only have a few seconds to consider my reaction. As Ben keeps saying, I don't want to cause a panic, but we can't act like everything is fine either. The parent chaperones might have information that can help us. Maybe they remember seeing Katy. Besides, now that the police are involved, it's only a matter of time before the truth comes out.

"One of our students was separated from the rest of her group. We don't want to cause a panic, but if you, or any of the other parents, have information that could help us, we'd appreciate it. Her name is Katy Callaway." I pull out my phone, zooming in on the class picture we took this morning. "Have you seen her? Maybe you could ask your son?"

The woman stares at the photo. "I don't remember seeing

her today. But I know the girl's mother. My goodness, she must be a nervous wreck."

I've not paused long enough to think about the mother's reaction. I'm not sure if she's even been told, or who should tell her. Will it be the school or the police? Regardless, the best way I can help right now is staying focused on Katy.

"Please tell us if you think of anything."

"Maybe I could help you look? I can get some of the other parents involved."

"Right now, it's best to keep everyone in one location," I say. "The local police are sending over a squad car right now to help with the search."

"The police." The woman puts a hand to her chest, then looks back in the direction of the children. Getting the police involved makes this situation more real and more... frightening.

As I walk further into the pavilion, I see other parents walking in my direction. I keep my head down, trying to avoid them. The remaining unsupervised children are gathered around playing with the pumpkins they collected from the patch.

I catch sight of Claire in the corner between two boys. I walk over to her and kiss the top of her head.

"Is it time to go to the playground?" she asks.

"Not yet. Mommy needs to work a little bit longer."

At least Claire, and the other children, seem unfazed. They've not yet been inflicted by the panic settling in with all the adults.

When I find Laura, still sitting at the same picnic table where we left her, my heart breaks. Ashen skin, blank stare. Regret and worry etched into the lines of her face. In all the years we've worked together, I can't remember a time where she's looked so distraught.

Actually, there is one other time I've seen her this upset, a moment I'd prefer to forget. It's when I told her I was pregnant.

David and I had agreed to keep it a secret until we reached the thirteen-week mark, but that was difficult to do around my co-workers, especially Laura. Her own daughter was pregnant, and she often talked about how excited she was to be a grandmother. One day on our planning period, the two of us were alone and I told her my news.

She burst into tears.

"Laura, what's wrong?" I asked.

"I'm so happy for you," she said, but there was an unmistakable sadness in her voice. "I really am."

"Then what's wrong?"

"I haven't told anyone here yet. I haven't known what to say." She took a deep breath. "My daughter and her husband lost the baby."

I gasped, squeezing Laura a little tighter. "I'm so sorry. If I had known, I wouldn't have said anything."

"No, I want to be happy for you. I *am* happy for you. I'm still just very sad for them."

We spent the remainder of the planning period talking. By the end of the day, I'd discreetly shared what happened with our other colleagues, so that Laura wouldn't have to get into the conversation again. Once I was home, I ordered a bouquet of flowers so that she would know I was still thinking about her, even when we weren't at school.

The next day, she sent a text message to thank me. There was a picture of a beautiful bouquet of white roses, adorned with pink and blue ribbon, and a message:

Thank you for being such a good friend.

We've always been there for each other during our lowest moments, and yet I'm not sure there's ever been a situation this scary.

When Laura sees me walking over, her eyes light up. "Did you find her?"

"She wasn't at the animal barn." I hate to be the one to tell her. "The others haven't found her either, but it's a big property. She's probably gotten turned around somewhere. We'll find her."

"I can't believe this happened. I've been a teacher for over thirty years. I've never put a child in danger."

"We don't know she's in danger," I say, trying to be hopeful. "These things happen. One time, when Claire was younger, I lost sight of her at the grocery store. It scared me half to death. David ended up finding her by the game machines at the front."

Laura smiles at that, albeit painfully. "They're just children. You never know what they're thinking."

"Exactly. Just give it some time."

I think back to that day in the grocery store. I'd been eyeing different options in the frozen section, and when I turned around, she was gone. I thought she'd wandered over to the next aisle, where David was taking his time selecting the perfect flavor of ice cream. When I turned the corner and she wasn't there, my own heart froze.

She'd been out of sight for only a few seconds, and it was enough to leave me paralyzed with worry. But my husband remained calm. He instructed me to check all the aisles while he went straight to the manager at the front of the store. Before they could even make an announcement over the loudspeaker, David heard her crying next to one of the outdated pinball machines.

I'm not sure we would have found her so quickly if it weren't for David's composure. He was always the practical one, and I feel myself missing him now, in a different way than I do the rest of the time.

"What's that?" Laura stands, pointing in the direction of the parking lot. A squad car has just arrived, its emergency lights strobing. "Did they call the police?"

"I called them. We can't waste more time."

She sits down without saying anything. There's a faraway look in her eyes, as though she's trying to think of something—anything—that will take her out of this situation.

"I have grandchildren," she mumbles, twisting the gold wedding band on her finger. "I can't imagine something happening to one of them..."

"Don't think about them right now," I say, grasping her shaking hands. "This isn't your fault."

She looks down into her lap, as though she wants to say more, but lacks the strength.

"Laura, I need to ask you, how long has it been since you last saw Katy?"

"I told you. We were at the animal barn when I last saw her."

I approach the next part cautiously. "Ben said you looked frazzled earlier. Like maybe you'd lost sight of her for longer than you originally said. It makes sense that you'd lose track of time, especially during such a stressful situation."

I wait for Laura to say something, but she remains silent.

"Do you know how long it's been?"

"I'm not sure. I know there were other groups around. I assumed she was off with one of them. It's not until Ben and his students left that I realized everyone was accounted for... except Katy." She looks at me now, tears in her eyes. "We must find her. If something happens to that little girl, I don't think I'll ever forgive myself."

"We're going to find her."

"Emma?" It's Jack. He's standing behind me, a phone at his ear. "Are you the one that called the police?"

"Yeah. It was me."

"Anna is with them at the ticket booth," he says. "They asked for you to meet them there. All the parents and students need to remain here."

"Tell them I'm on my way."

I look back at Laura before walking in that direction.

ELEVEN

Brendan McCallister, the property owner, is in his sixties with gray hair and a full beard. He's wearing a plaid shirt tucked into jeans, his clothes appearing both worn and expensive, not the typical outfit you'd expect to see on a farmer. His daughter stands by his side, looking much less put-together. She's wearing leggings and a neon-green hoodie, her hair pulled back into a bun. She appears to have gotten dressed in a hurry, as though she received the news about a missing child and rushed to the property.

Ben, Anna and two local police officers round off the group standing by the ticket booth. I assume Ben and Anna already gave them most of the information, but they insisted on talking to me since I made the original call.

"So, we're not sure how long this child has been missing?" one of the officers asks.

"At least an hour," I say. "Maybe longer."

"It's easy for kids to lose their way at night. During the day, sometimes a parent will lose sight of a little one. Turns out the kid just ran off to another part of the property," McCallister says. "Usually, we find them in a couple of minutes. Can't say we've ever had one missing for this long."

"Where is the most likely place for a child to be?"

"Well, you said she's not in the barn or the playground. That leaves the cornfields. She wouldn't have made it over to the pumpkin patch without being spotted by one of my workers."

The first officer nods. "We'll take a few people over there and split up."

"I'll stay here at the front," the owner's daughter says, looking at the parking lot. "It looks like we might need some crowd control."

McCallister's Pumpkin Patch is closed to the public until evening, and yet there's a line of people building outside of the closed gate. Most of them are parents. The ones who weren't able to chaperone today's field trip. According to our schedule, the bus should have arrived back at the school by now. They're likely wondering where their children are. And even though we've kept the remaining parents together, we have no control over their phones. Word must have gotten out that a child is missing.

"We can't let anyone on the property," says the officer.

"I'm on it," the daughter says, tramping toward the gates.

"Let's gather the others at the pavilion," the first officer says. "I can question the teacher involved, then we'll head for the cornfields."

Shouting voices carry over from the direction of the parking lot. An argument has broken out between the owner's daughter and one of the parents. When I look closer, I recognize the woman.

It's Danica Callaway, Katy's mother.

I rush to them.

"Emma? I got a phone call from the school. They told me no

one can find Katy." She sounds distraught. "Tell me that isn't true."

"It's a big property. She's probably lost. We have tons of people helping to find her."

"You have to let me in there. She's my baby. You have to let me help find my baby."

"We can't do that. The police have told us no one can be let in or out. This is what's best for her. It will keep her safe."

"I trusted the school to keep her safe!" Her sadness morphs into anger. "You were supposed to be watching her!"

"I know. You have to trust when I say everyone is doing their best to find her—"

"Don't you get it? She isn't missing. *He* took her."

"Who?"

"Jasper. My ex. We're in the middle of custody agreements, and he's decided to take her."

"Have you talked to him today?"

"He's not answering his calls, but he never does. I swear to God, if he has her—"

"He wasn't here today. She came on the trip without a parent."

"How do you know he didn't enter later in the day? He could have taken her away before you even realized it!"

As much as I want to keep Danica calm, I realize there might be some truth in what she has to say. The place wasn't on lockdown until we realized Katy was missing. Could Jasper Callaway have snuck onto the premises and taken his daughter without any of us realizing?

"You need to get a hold of him," I tell her. "Have the police contact him, if you must. If Katy is with him, we need to know."

She takes out her phone and starts pounding in numbers. She pauses and looks at me.

"Who was with her when she went missing? I want to know who was supposed to be watching my daughter."

I keep seeing Laura's broken face. She's eaten up with guilt, and I know she isn't strong enough to handle this type of attack.

"I was," I lie. "Katy was with me."

Danica looks shocked at my answer. She was hoping to have someone else to blame.

"I will never forgive you if something happens to her," she says. "You have no business being around children."

"I'm sorry, Danica. I promise, I'm not going to leave until we know what's happened."

But Danica is no longer listening. She's collapsed to the ground. The woman standing behind her—Is she a friend? Family member?—wraps her arms around her, trying to comfort her. The whole scene is too hard to watch. I start walking back to the pavilion.

"You better find her!" Danica yells after me.

I face ahead, too upset to look back.

It's hard witnessing Danica's pain, because I know that what she is saying is true.

We're all to blame for not keeping her daughter safe.

TWELVE

Back at the pavilion, we're trying to spread information to the rest of the staff, while simultaneously warding off questions from parents. Jack and Anna move from one parent to the next, looking flustered. The presence of police officers has, understandably, piqued their interest, and we can see the growing crowds of people lining up near the ticket booth.

Sarah walks toward me, her phone to her ear. When she gets closer, she ends the call and looks at the parents crowding the pavilion. Some are starting to stand and pace around, visibly agitated.

"This is turning into a shitshow," Sarah says, watching with morbid curiosity.

"I know, but we won't know how serious this is until we've looked everywhere." I nod to her phone. "Was that the school?"

She blushes and looks away. "No. It was... someone else."

Darren. The last thing she needs is to be worried about him when there is an actual crisis taking place.

"We're all under stress, but I need you to stay focused. There's no telling how bad this could get, okay?"

"You're right." Her face hardens. "You think it could be worse than her being lost?"

I look around to make sure no one can hear me. "Danica Callaway seems to think her ex-husband might have taken her."

"My goodness. I remember you said their divorce hearings were ugly, but this?"

"You never know how a parent is going to react when they think they might lose custody," I say. "And I hate to say this, but if he didn't take her, there's always the possibility that someone else did."

"You think she could have been kidnapped?"

"I don't know. There were a lot of people who left before we realized she was missing. And Laura isn't being very clear about how long she was gone."

Sarah shivers a little as she rests her palms against her forehead. "This stress is too much for me. I don't know how you're holding it together."

I think of that day back in the grocery store. I was the nervous wreck, while David kept a clear head. I smile at the thought that, maybe, some of his level-headedness rubbed off on me, in the short amount of time we had together.

Jack wanders closer to me, whispers so that no one can hear.

"The parents keep asking me questions," he says. "I don't know what to say."

"Reassure them that everything is fine, and if they have any information that could be useful, direct them to one of the police officers standing by the gate."

He nods and exhales. "Have you ever dealt with something like this before?"

"No, I haven't."

It isn't until then that I consider how terrifying this must be for the likes of Anna and Jack. They're new to the profession, just trying to get some experience under their belts, and they've been thrown into a situation even veteran teachers would dread.

"Look," I say, facing both Anna and Jack. "Right now, we're all scared because we don't know what's happening. But this is just like every other day. We keep our kids safe, at all costs."

"Okay. Treat it like any other day," he says, trying to sound confident. Anna nods, but I can't help noticing that her face seems drained of all color.

"Look after Laura, too," I add. "She's handling this worse than all of us."

An officer brushes past, standing in front of me to better address the people standing beneath the pavilion.

"Okay, parents and students. I need everyone's attention," he yells, waving his scrawny arms in the air. "We're going to relocate this group to the playground down the hill. We need to get away from the crowds waiting at the gate."

"Tell us what is going on," one parent shouts.

"You can't just force us to stay here," another yells. "Some of us need to leave."

"We've got an officer placed at all the exits," the policeman says. "No one is leaving until we say it's safe. Is that clear?"

The parents don't say anything to this. They only grumble as they stand and gather their belongings, ushering their children down the hill.

"Mommy, are we going to the playground?"

Claire walks up to me and holds my hand. Another spasm of guilt strikes my chest. This was supposed to be our fun day together. My six-year-old daughter still has no idea of the severity of the situation we're in, and all she wants is her mother's undivided attention, something I'm not able to give.

But then I think of Danica Callaway and the pain she's enduring at this very moment. I think of Katy, lost and alone, or worse. She needs as much help as she can get right now.

I bend down so that I'm at eye level with Claire and kiss her cheek.

"Listen, I know I've not been able to spend as much time

with you as I wanted today, but Mommy is doing something really, really important. Wait with Ms. Green just a little while longer."

"But you promised we'd go to the playground."

"You get to go with your friends, just not with me. Not right now."

"It'll be okay, Claire," Sarah says, walking up on our conversation. "Mommy will be back as soon as she can."

"I just wanted to spend the day with you."

"Hey, we're still going to carve jack-o'-lanterns, right? We can even come back to the pumpkin patch this weekend, if you want."

"Okay."

She doesn't sound particularly devastated or pleased. Just the normal state of settling I feel like I'm always leaving her in.

"Hey, don't beat yourself up," Sarah says, when she sees the disappointment on my face. "And don't worry about Claire. The minute she gets on the swing set, she'll forget all about you." She laughs. "I meant that in the best possible way."

"I know." I watch as the swarm of parents and students make their way down the hill. "Just keep an eye on her. And try to keep the rest of the parents and students calm."

"I will."

I take one more look at Claire as she makes a run for the swings, wishing I could be beside her, but I can't.

I must leave my child behind so that I can help find someone else's.

THIRTEEN

The owner leads the way to the fields, shouting out orders.

"There are two mazes," McCallister explains. "The one on the left is the harder one. The one on the right we designed to be easier, for the kids."

"But if she wandered in there by herself, she could have gone into the wrong one," Ben says.

"Which is why we need to check both," the officer says. He looks back at the owner. "You know the area the best. Where do you suggest we start?"

"If you're really lost, you could be out in these things for hours. They run for more than a mile, depending on what route you take. I say three of us take the bigger one, while the other two take the small one."

"Let's go," the officer says, marching toward the field on the left.

"I'll stick with them in case we find anything," Anna says. "We all have each other's numbers."

"I guess that leaves us together again," I say to Ben.

"Let's go."

It's amazing how quickly the cornstalks swallow you whole.

At the entrance of the maze, you think it can't be that bad, but after a few minutes of walking, all I can see are tall golden stalks and the hard ground beneath them. Retracing my steps at this point seems easy, but with so much on my mind, I can't be sure. It's understandable how Katy, or any child, could get lost in here.

"Should we stick together?" I ask Ben.

"Maybe, at first. Yeah."

He sounds unsure, something I'm not used to hearing. It's strange how this situation has brought out different sides of us all. Ben, who is so confident he borders on arrogance, has become fickle. Jack and Anna are helpful as ever, but they're clearly shaken, as though this very situation might make them change career paths entirely. Laura, always composed and professional, is crumbling beneath the magnitude of this one mistake.

And then there's me. I've taken the reins more than I would have thought, more than I did that day I lost my own daughter. It would be nice to say I learned from that experience, but if I'm being honest, I haven't had much choice about being a leader in recent years.

"How long have we been out here?" Ben asks.

"I'm not sure." I look at my watch, even though I don't have a clue what time it was when we entered the cornfields. "Maybe twenty minutes?"

"No one has contacted us. That means they haven't found her."

"According to the map, we've not even made it to the center of the fields yet."

"But we're losing daylight. The sun will start setting in less than an hour. If we don't find her before nightfall..."

His sentence trails off. None of us want to consider what not finding her means. It's not like we can hold the remaining parents and students hostage. Eventually, we'll have to let them leave and expand our search efforts. We might even have to come to terms with the idea Katy didn't just wander off; something more sinister could have happened. None of us want to think of those possibilities, and yet every passing minute brings us closer to confronting them.

I think of Danica, likely still being restrained by the ticket booth. For a moment, I hope her theory is correct. Maybe Jasper Callaway did find his way onto the property. Maybe he and his daughter are having burgers and ice cream at this very moment, unaware of the drama their absence has caused. At least in that case we'd know where she is. We'd know she's safe. I still can't fathom a parent hurting his own child. Then again, there have been far too many instances that prove me wrong.

"We need to split up," Ben says, after another several minutes of searching. "There's no other way to cover all this land."

"Are you sure? The police officer didn't say anything about splitting up. It might be smarter to stick together."

"We both have cell phones and full service. If we find anything important, we'll call each other."

He doesn't give me any time to argue. He charges left, and within seconds he's swallowed whole by the cornstalks. Only the crunching sound of boots lets me know I'm not alone.

"Oh, Katy. Where are you?" I say under my breath. I imagine the wind can carry my words onward, and that my question will be answered like a prayer. Minutes slip through my fingers like liquid. Too much time is passing.

A strange feeling takes hold when you realize all might be lost. Usually, people go through life experiencing nothing more than close calls. Very rarely does the feeling of complete hopelessness consume you.

But I know that feeling, live with it every day, and I'm feeling the sensation even heavier now, like something awful is waiting around the next turn.

When David died, there was no rush to the hospital, pleading with doctors or moments of prayer. By the time the officers arrived at my door to tell me about the accident, he was already gone.

In an instant, I was a widow, a single parent, a woman living without hope.

And Claire was still the same little girl. Much like today's crisis, she had no true understanding of what had happened, that the father she loved and admired was gone. At only four years old, her grief came later, in unpredictable moments. When David wasn't there to read her a bedtime story. Or on Christmas morning, when she'd rush downstairs to greet us, and find only me. Or at the beginning of the school year, when Laura instructed her students to draw a picture of their family. Claire's drawing featured the two of us in matching dresses, standing in front of our house. Daddy hovered above us in the sky, a pair of wings drawn on his back. Seeing that image was heartbreaking, trying to grasp what a loss like that must do to a young child.

Grief is a hard beast to fight, mainly because it stays alongside you the rest of your life. An unwanted companion. At best, I keep the misery away, but in uncertain moments like this, when I feel a fresh, new wave of heartache rising, all the feelings return.

There's a sound nearby. What it is, exactly, is hard to describe. It's not the same forceful crunch I heard as Ben stomped away, but I call out to him anyway, wondering if he's there.

"Ben? Is that you?" I wait. "Have you found anything?"

There's no response. I keep moving forward, deeper into the maze, when I hear it again. It's a soft sound, like a whimpering.

My mind goes back to the animals in the barn. They appear playful when behind the security of the gates. But this is still, in many ways, the wilderness. Could there be other animals on this land? Could they be dangerous? If so, I hope Katy hasn't encountered one.

I hear the sound again, and realize I'm getting closer to it.

"Katy?"

I've reverted back to the impossible. I'm only *hoping* I heard her. But when the sound continues, I think maybe, just maybe...

"Katy?" I say again, willing my voice to sound less frightened.

"Ms. Howard?"

At the next turn, I see her. She's crying, huddled up in between the cornstalks, a can of soda in her hand. I grab her with such force that I knock the drink from her grip, and the liquid splashes onto both of us.

"My goodness, Katy. Are you okay? Are you hurt?"

I wonder if, like a person lost in the desert, this is nothing more than a mirage. I wonder if the stress of searching and having no answers has made my mind deteriorate. And yet, when I wrap my arms around Katy, she's solid. Her skin is cold, and yet holding her fills me with a joy, thankfulness, warmth.

"Are you okay?" I repeat.

"I got lost," she says. Her voice is raw. "I was scared."

"It's okay," I say, squeezing her closer to me. "We've found you now."

My chest feels as though it will burst, and the only way to keep that from happening is to open my own mouth and shout.

"She's here!" I exclaim. "Katy is safe. We found her!"

I feel my eyes watering as I let those beautiful words sink in.

FOURTEEN

I send out a message in the group chat letting everyone know she's been found, but don't take time to read any of the responses. All of my attention is devoted to Katy.

From what I can tell, she isn't injured, but she's shaken. She's a six-year-old girl who has been lost for over two hours. I can only imagine how frightened she must be.

"Am I in trouble?" she asks, once the tears have subsided and she's gained control of her voice.

"No, sweetheart. We're just happy you're okay."

A conversation about sticking with the group can be had later. Right now, I'm just relieved. All the dark possibilities that had entered my mind have disappeared.

"I was scared."

"I know you were, honey." Instinctively, I rock her back and forth, the same way I comfort Claire when she's upset about something. "Are you sure you aren't hurt?"

"I couldn't find my way out of the corn. It all looked the same."

"Did you hear us calling your name?"

She nods her head.

"Why didn't you say anything?"

"I don't know." She rests her head on her knees, closing into herself, as though she's about to start crying again.

I can't judge her reaction. Most children tend to freeze when faced with fear. So much time passed, she was probably concerned she'd be in some sort of trouble. In fact, that was her first question to me.

It's hard to understand the way a child thinks, but we can all relate to being scared, and the comfort of feeling safe. All I want for Katy is to know she is protected.

Ben is the first to reach us.

"Is she okay?"

"A little shocked, but perfectly healthy."

Ben laughs, for the first time since we arrived. That hearty chuckle that puts everyone around him at ease. "You scared us a little bit, Miss Katy."

"I'm sorry."

"Don't apologize." He scoops her up in one swift movement and starts walking in the direction of the exit. "Let's get you out of here."

"Do you know where you're going?"

"I have a good sense of direction. I'm just glad she hadn't wandered any farther in."

When we exit our maze, the second search group is waiting for us. Anna comes running up to Katy and gives her a hug. Like me, she has teary eyes and a wide smile.

"I'm so happy we found you," she says. "I know Ms. Bailey will be happy to see you."

"Where is Ms. Bailey?" Katy asks.

"She's near the entrance, with everyone else," I say. "They'll all be so happy to see you."

Katy smiles at this, the trauma of the past couple of hours erasing. That's the good thing about children. They move past things far easier than adults do. Even though we've found her, I sense I'll have trouble sleeping tonight. All of us will.

"I'm going to head back," Ben says. "We're going to have a line of parents ready to leave."

"I'll join you," Anna says, skipping after him.

"Can I ask you a few questions, sweetheart?" the officer says, bending down to speak with Katy.

He likely wants to get a statement before we return to the chaos of the pavilion and parking lot. The officer asks her the same questions I did back in the cornfield, but Katy is even more reluctant to answer. She keeps squeezing my hand, grateful to be around someone she knows. This man is a stranger, and he doesn't get much out of her other than *I got lost* and *I was scared.*

"Have a sip of this," the owner says, handing over a water bottle. Katy takes it and begins to drink.

The officer makes a call over his radio, announcing that the child has been found and is safe. I can hear people cheering, even though we are on the other side of the property.

"Ready to head back?" I ask her.

Katy nods, continuing to hold my hand as we head towards the exit.

FIFTEEN

As we make it over the hill, I can see there's a long line of people waiting to leave the property.

A woman comes rushing up to us. It's Laura.

"Is it true? Did you find her?"

The question is answered when Katy pokes out from behind me. Laura falls to her knees, embracing her.

"I'm so sorry I took my eyes off you," she says. She's crying hard. I can only imagine how heavy the guilt she was carrying must have felt, and how relieved she must be to have it lifted.

Laura stands and looks at me. "I'm just so happy. I'd worried myself sick."

"I think we could all use some rest." I check my watch to see that it's nearing four o'clock, long past the time we should have returned to school. "What should we do about the buses?"

"Sarah stayed behind with the unchaperoned students. It's my understanding all their parents are here. I'll meet them at the front and start signing them out. The others have already headed back to the school." She pauses. "I couldn't leave until I saw her again. I needed to know she was okay."

Before I can say anything else, Laura takes off. I'm pleased to see she's quickly returned to teacher mode. I hope this situation hasn't traumatized her too much. It was a mistake any of us could have made, and I know Laura to be a good teacher. A good person.

Katy still hasn't let go of my hand. We walk straight to the front of the ticket line, the officer and Mr. McCallister following behind us.

I'm sure Danica was the first person to know that Katy had been found, but I can only imagine the tension building inside of her, none of it really mattering until she can hold her child again. When she sees us, she pushes back the officer at the front, and runs to us.

"Oh, Katy," she cries. "I'm so happy to see you."

Tears flow freely as the mother and daughter embrace. I'm happy to witness their reunion. It appears I've shared little glimpses of everyone's fears in the past couple of hours, so it's nice to join in their relief, too.

A man walks up behind them. I recognize him as Jasper Callaway, Katy's father. The three of them embrace, and for a moment, whatever animosity lies between them no longer exists. They're a family again, rejoicing in the simple gift of being together.

Danica stands slowly and looks at me.

"Thank you so much."

"Trust me, I'm relieved, too," I say.

"I'm so sorry for how I spoke to you earlier. I was just so angry, but you—"

"It's okay." I don't need to hear her apologies. Danica was in a position no parent wants to be in. "Katy is safe. That's all that matters."

I walk in the direction of the playground, a huge wave of exhaustion washing over me. I think I'd kept so many feelings at bay during the search to find Katy, and now they're hitting me all at once. Nervousness. Panic. Fear. Relief. Gratitude.

We take for granted how glorious it can be to have a normal, boring day. It's not until tragedy strikes that we fully appreciate the happiness of a mundane existence.

Sarah comes running up to me, and like most everyone else, she is crying.

"Thank God, we found her," I say. "I can safely say that's the scariest thing that's ever happened to me on the job."

But Sarah doesn't say anything. In fact, she's looking around me, her eyes searching the area, even though I'm standing right in front of her.

"Sarah, did you hear me? I just returned Katy to her parents. She's perfectly fine."

She opens her mouth to speak, but her lips tremble. She takes a deep breath and starts again.

"Emma, I'm so sorry."

"Sorry about what?"

She clenches her fists, working up the nerve to say it. "I can't find Claire."

SIXTEEN

It takes a moment to process what she's said.

I've just come down from the high of finding Katy, of seeing her reunited with her parents. And it isn't registering why Sarah isn't as happy as everyone else.

Then the reality of her words settles in.

"What do you mean you can't find her?"

"I... I was with her and the other parents in the playground. There were so many kids running around, and I thought she was in one of the tunnels—"

I don't let her finish before sprinting off in that direction. A couple of parents and their children pass as I make my way to the sand mounds at the playground's center. By now, almost everyone is gone. I can count the remaining people on two hands.

I jump to the ground, ducking my head inside one of the rubber tubes and shout.

"Claire?"

Only my echo responds.

I stand quickly, marching to another, hoping my voice will carry through the interconnecting underground tubes.

"Claire? Are you in there?" Nothing. "If you can hear me, you better come out right now."

"I've already tried looking for her." Sarah's voice comes from behind me. "I even sent some of the kids into the tunnels, but they said it was empty."

The swing set in front of us is empty, as is the staircase leading toward the slides. I turn, looking behind me at the pavilion. Also empty.

"Sarah, where is she? She was with your group."

"When word got back that you'd found Katy, the officer told parents they were free to leave. Ben came to fetch my other students, and that's when I realized she wasn't with us."

"You didn't see her before that?"

"Of course I did. She was running around playing with all the others. But I don't know where she is now."

The panic from earlier reclaims me. An icy sensation starts in my chest, spreading out through my remaining limbs, like frost. I start running in the direction of the entrance. The only face I recognize is Laura's. She's holding a clipboard, in conversation with one of the parents.

"Have you seen Claire?"

"She's back at the playground with Sarah," she says, calmly. Her expression changes when she sees the panic on my face, and Sarah standing behind me. "Isn't she?"

"I can't find her," Sarah says, pulling on the sleeves of her jacket. "I thought maybe she wandered up here with one of the other kids."

"I haven't seen her." Laura looks at me, her expression difficult to read.

"What about the others? Maybe she's with Jack or Ben?"

"They've already left," Laura says. "Anna, too."

Which means the only people here that Claire has any connection with are the three of us, and none of us have seen her.

I spot one of the officers standing by the entrance, the one from the other search party. I rush over to him.

"Officer, I can't find my daughter."

"What do you mean you can't find your daughter?" he says. "You're one of the teachers, right?"

"Yes. My daughter was on today's field trip, and I left her behind with one of my colleagues so I could join the search."

"How old is she?"

"Six. Like all the others."

A shadow crosses his face, as though he's seen a ghost. We've all just gone through the stress of finding one child, and now another one is missing. *My child* is missing.

"Where's the last place you saw her?"

"She was at the playground with me," Sarah speaks up. "She was playing with the other kids, and then she was just... gone."

Laura is standing nearby. She pulls out her phone. "I'll call Anna. Maybe Claire headed back with one of the other teachers by mistake."

She's trying to be helpful, but the odds of that are slim. Still, I'll take slim odds over not knowing where my daughter is. Less than an hour ago, she was standing right beside me. I was pinching her cheeks, promising to take her to the playground.

The officer turns his back to us and says something into his radio. When he turns, his brow is furrowed. "We have a few officers in the parking lot helping direct traffic. They're going to come over and help us look around. She's probably just lost her way in all the chaos. We'll cross back over to the corn maze, if we have to."

"We just came from that direction. We would have passed her," I say.

Laura puts her phone into her pocket, her balance unsteady. "She's not at the school. None of them remember seeing her before they left."

"Maybe she's back at the animal barn?" Sarah suggests, hopeful.

Just then, Mr. McCallister comes walking up. He's carrying a metal bucket filled with feed. "My workers closed up the barn before we entered the cornfields." He puts down the bucket. "What's going on here?"

It's as though I've entered an alternate universe, the horror of this day on an unending loop.

"It's my daughter. We can't find her."

"She wouldn't be over there. Or the pumpkin patches. I've had people watching both since the first little girl went missing." The man is, understandably, irritated, but then he sees the panic on my face, and a wave of compassion washes over him. "Do you have a picture of your daughter, ma'am? Maybe I remember seeing her."

I quickly take out my phone and pull up a picture. It's the same photo we took this morning, the one I showed officers earlier when we were looking for Katy, but this time I zoom in on a different face. One that looks so much like my own.

"Wait, this one is better," I say, swiping over to the selfie we took while we were in the pumpkin patch. It's a close-up of the two of us, capturing her smiling face. "Her name is Claire. She's only six, and there's no way she'd wander off by herself."

"That's what was said about the other little girl, right?" the officer says.

"This is different."

Katy Callaway is outgoing and spunky. Claire is sensitive and reserved. I never would have guessed Katy had the bravery to wander into a corn maze by herself, but I know my daughter. She wouldn't wander away from Sarah, or any other adult, unless she was looking for me.

Then again, there was that day at the grocery store. She wandered off then, but she was only three at the time. She's older now, smarter. More careful.

"You need to listen to me," I say, trembling. "If she's not with one of us, something is very, very wrong."

"Try to stay calm," the officer says.

But the terror in my voice only increases. "All the places we were searching for Katy are already roped off. Claire wouldn't have a chance to get into those places if she tried."

"We've got officers making their way over here right now to help look."

The officers in the parking lot helping to direct traffic. *Traffic.* It sinks in that all the people we asked to stay in place while we were searching for Katy have left. Anyone that might have seen her. Anyone that might have *taken* her.

"What if she's not here?" I begin to shout. "What if she's gone with one of them?"

"We're going to start looking," the officer says, but his voice fades out.

"Oh my gosh, Emma. I'm so sorry," Sarah cries, but her voice wavers, too.

I feel myself falling, unfazed by the hard ground beneath my buckling knees. I'm too consumed by questions and terror and grief.

She could be anywhere. With anyone. My daughter is gone.

SEVENTEEN

Step Two: Get Away.

As I drive down the street, each passing car captures my attention, makes me want to ask questions. Do they know what I've done? Have they figured out she is missing? No, each person has their eyes forward, staring at the stop sign or car or stoplight ahead. People tend to only see what's in front of them, don't take much notice of what's around them.

I check the rearview mirror. I can hardly tell she's there. She's covered with blankets and jackets. Silent. If I can make it to the house, the second step will be complete. We just might get away.

The hardest part was convincing her to drink. She kept saying she wasn't thirsty and that it tasted funny, but eventually she listened, because that's what little girls have been trained to do; they listen to adults like me.

She was knocked out before we even made it on the highway. It was a kindness, what I did. I'm not trying to scare her. This isn't about that. This is about taking what I finally need from life. It's my turn to feel whole again, after countless months of being broken.

Dr. Meade knows about my past, of course, but she doesn't fixate on the early years, like all the other shrinks I know. Every other doctor I talked to wanted to travel too far back, examine my childhood.

I don't like thinking about that time in my life, and I don't think it has anything to do with the person I am today. To say otherwise gives my parents too much credit.

Sure, my childhood was complicated, but unoriginally so. Dad was a drunk. Abusive. Most drunks have a loveable side, a person worth loving before the booze takes over. My dad was miserable sober, and the bottle only made him worse.

Mom tired of his behavior and tried to avoid him. If I'd had a choice, I would have done the same, but you don't get many choices when you're a child. She was always gone. Dad said she was out sleeping around. For years, I wondered what that phrase meant. I had these images of my mother dozing off in random places. Behind her desk at work, in line at the grocery store, on the bench waiting for the bus.

Once I was old enough to understand what he meant, I didn't much care about either one of them. Even now, it's hard to tell what came first. Mom's men or Dad's drinking.

All my old doctors kept wanting to focus on these details, as though the secret to my sickness started way back then. But it didn't. I had a normal life once. Even a chance at a happy one.

But it didn't work out.

My foot is tapping against the floorboard, my hands starting to sweat. Dr. Meade says it's important to identify negative thought patterns and avoid them. I have to leave my past where it belongs if I ever want to have a brighter future. Sometimes I wonder if I ever would have made it this far without Dr. Meade's help.

We make it to the house, and I carry Claire inside, straight through the wood-paneled living room and down the stairs, into the basement. She won't be here long, but I still tried to make it *comfortable for her. A mattress on the floor, a clean blanket to keep her warm. Most importantly, she has me. Someone to love her and keep her safe.*

It's not much, but it's better than what some kids get. More than I ever got.

EIGHTEEN

EMMA

After David died, my doctor gave me a prescription of anxiety medication. I have a small dose I take daily, and I can take another when on the verge of a panic attack. Very few times in the past two years have I felt the need to take it. Very few times have I *been able* to take it. I've not had a choice about feeling what I'm feeling; I've only had the option to push through the pressure and stress, for Claire. She's needed me.

Thankfully, I've continued to carry the medication with me, just in case. Twenty minutes ago, I asked Sarah to fish one of the pills out for me. Just now, I'm feeling the calming effects kick in, my bloodstream fizzing.

And yet the other feelings remain. The shock and worry and confusion. In my twelve years as a teacher, I've never had a child go missing. Not truly missing, the way it unfolded today with Katy. And now Claire.

Every time I think her name, every time her face appears in my mind, I want to double over and cry. I'm seated under the pavilion, Sarah and Laura at my side, being watched by one of the officers. He assures me that they are searching every place

Claire could have wandered off to in such a short amount of time, but his assurances don't satisfy me.

Much like Danica Callaway at the gate two hours ago, I'm not permitted to help search this time. It doesn't bother me that I can't assist. It's not because I don't want to help find her. It's because I can't face the wrenching disappointment of looking somewhere and finding it empty. I need my daughter to come back to me.

"Excuse me, are you Emma?"

A woman approaches me. She's wearing a dark trench coat which is belted tightly across her waist. Her hair is pulled back into a low bun, her eyes study my face.

I stand up. "Yes."

"I'm Vera Sanchez. I'm a detective with the North Ridge Police Department. I understand your daughter is the one that's missing."

"Yes." It's difficult to speak, so I clear my throat. "I'm a teacher at the school. One of our students was lost during the field trip, so I went searching for her. When I returned, she was gone."

"Yes, I'm aware of the earlier incident." She smiles tightly. "Do you have a picture of your daughter?"

I pull out my phone and share the selfie we took in the pumpkin patch.

"This is good. It lets us know what she's wearing," the detective says. "Do you have another picture? Something I can send out."

I scroll through my photo library, my stomach clenching with each picture I pass. I pause on her fall school picture. Detective Sanchez gives me her number, and I send it.

"Thank you. This will be very helpful," she says, putting her phone back in her jacket pocket. "Walk me through everything that happened leading up to your daughter's disappearance."

I begin from the moment Katy went missing, explaining my attempts to find her, and that I left Claire with Sarah. At this point, the detective directs her questions to her, and I listen as the same information is exchanged repeatedly.

"Why are you here?" I ask. I don't realize I've interrupted until I see the strange look on Sanchez's face.

"I'm sorry?"

"I mean, when Katy was reported missing, they only sent out a squad car. You said you're a detective."

She nods now, understanding my train of thought.

"I'm afraid this situation is a little different. When the first girl was reported missing, the scene was relatively closed off. It's my understanding there were several groups able to start looking for her right away."

"Yes. I was with one of them."

"We're no longer dealing with a secure scene. Most of the people who were on the premises have already left, and Claire could be with any one of them."

"You're saying you think someone took her?" Laura asks. I can barely think the words, let alone say them.

"There's one more group searching a remote part of the property. I'm waiting to hear back."

"But you don't think she got lost?" I ask. "You think someone took her."

"The grounds were covered extensively during the search for the first girl, and we've had farm staff and police officers monitoring it ever since."

"Clearly not that closely," I say. "My daughter *is* missing."

Sanchez smiles tightly again. "But it seems likely someone would have seen her. If not right away, then definitely in the time since you reported her missing. She could have followed another parent into the parking lot. A friend, maybe. Is there anyone you can call?"

"I can't think of any parents she would feel comfortable leaving with."

"So she could have wandered off, sure. Maybe she's even off the property, and that's why we've not been able to locate her," she says. "But I'm afraid we need to be as careful as possible until we rule out foul play."

"Foul play?" The words sit painfully on my tongue.

"If there is foul play involved, I'm afraid the person who took Claire used Katy's disappearance to their advantage."

"Wait, you're saying you think someone did this on purpose? You think they took the opportunity to abduct Claire while everyone else was focused on Katy?"

While I was focused on Katy, I think. My own daughter was taken, and I wasn't there.

"It's a possibility. And given the circumstances, we need to act fast. The parking lot wasn't monitored after Katy was found, which means if someone did take her off the grounds, there was no one watching to stop them."

The seriousness of the situation sinks in. I see all the faces around me, the way they're looking at me with shock and horror and sadness. Then I think of Claire's face. Innocent and pure, wanting nothing more than to spend the day with her mother.

I go to take a seat, but I slip. I'm falling, and I'm not sure when I'll find the strength to stand back up.

NINETEEN

Detective Sanchez drives me away from McCallister's Pumpkin Patch. We don't speak. I lean my head against the cool glass of the car window. The sky was an inky blue when we left the patch. Now, it's a heavy gray. Soon, it will be black. Night. And my daughter isn't with me.

"Some officers will meet us at your house," she says. "They'll want to search the place. Maybe set up in case any calls come in."

"Calls?"

"In situations like this, the kidnapper might try to reach out to you."

The kidnapper.

A horrifying word. Much worse than any other monster I could have conjured up—a villain, a vampire, a creep. A kidnapper is real, and it's my child that's in his grasp. My stomach flips, and my body lurches forward.

"I think I'm going to be sick."

Without speaking, Sanchez rolls down the passenger side window. The sounds from outside break into the quiet car, the wind tangling my hair and cooling my cheeks. I take in several deep breaths. *Stay focused*, I tell myself. Claire needs me now more than ever.

I close my eyes, trying to picture every detail of her. Her pale skin, covered in amber freckles. The missing tooth on the bottom row. Her silky blonde hair. I keep my eyes closed, focusing on these details, until the car stops.

When I open my eyes, my house stands before me. Two-story brick, shaped like a perfect square. There's a white wrap-around porch that runs the length of the house. The roof is black metal, a purchase David and I saved over two years to afford. An investment for our future, we had said. Now everything is so uncertain.

Without thinking, I get out of the car, walk up the concrete porch steps I never got around to painting. I run through the bottom level of the house, turning on every light. I rush up the creaky wooden staircase, heading straight for the master bedroom, then for Claire's bedroom. However unlikely, I need to search.

Maybe she wasn't taken. Maybe she simply lost her way. Maybe she hitched a ride with another parent, and they forgot to tell me. Maybe her disappearance *is* easily explained, and the aching panic of the past hour means nothing. Desperate, I'll believe any scenario, no matter how unlikely.

Those thoughts vanish when I look at Claire's empty bed. She isn't here. She never was.

All that remains are her belongings. Each item speaks to me, it seems, telling me a different story about my daughter. Her beige baby blanket with an embroidered lion in the center, which she still sleeps with, even now, is crumpled on top of her comforter. The easel in the corner of the room speaks to her creativity, brings back memories of her drawing and coloring. I'm reminded of the argument we had this morning when I see the hairbrush on her dresser, and I wince with regret. Had I known the direction our day would take, I never would have been frustrated over something as unimportant as a hair ribbon.

"Anything look out of place?" It's Sanchez's voice behind me.

"No." Then, without being able to stop myself. "She isn't here."

"Is there someone we can call? Your husband—"

"My husband is dead."

I sit on the bed. Finally, for the first time since we left the pumpkin patch, the tears come. My breaths are hot and heavy. My thoughts, the room, the whole world spin around me. I've lost everything.

Then, a hand.

"I'm sorry." Sanchez offers her condolences. For my husband or my daughter, I'm not sure. "Is there anyone else we can call? Any other family?"

"We have no other family." After several seconds of silence, I say, "I'll call Sarah. She was with me at the pumpkin patch."

"She's the one who was with your daughter when she went missing?"

"Yes."

As though I need reminding. But she's also my closest friend, and it hurts too much being alone. I can hear the police officers arriving downstairs, their heavy footsteps against the hardwood. Despite their presence, the house feels empty.

"Is there a landline in the house?" Sanchez asks. I nod. She looks into the hallway. "We'll tap the line, see if—"

She's cut off by the sound of a phone ringing. It's not the house phone, it's my cell, ringing in the distance. I left it downstairs.

I hurry down, Sanchez close behind me, following the muffled ringtone. By the time I find my purse and dig out my phone, the call is lost.

"I don't know the number," I say out loud, defeated. Was

this my chance? Someone calling with information? Someone calling to say she's been found?

Within seconds, the phone blares again. Another call.

"Who is it?" Sanchez asks.

"Another unknown number." Quickly, I answer, bringing the phone to my ear. "Hello?"

"Is this Emma?"

"Yes."

"This is Rick Richards with WATE news in North Ridge. I'm calling to see if there is any information you can give us about your daughter. Would you like to make a comment?"

"A comment—"

Before I can finish my sentence, let alone a thought, Sanchez has snatched the phone from my hand.

"Who did you say this is?" She bites her lip, nodding. "Tell your producer all other calls to this line will be interference with an ongoing investigation."

She hangs up and hands the phone back to me.

"The news stations already know Claire is missing," I say, staring ahead blankly. "I thought it was someone who might be able to help."

"My team will make sure to reach out to all local news. We want to keep your line open, in case any important calls do come through." She looks at another officer entering the house, watches as the uniformed man climbs the stairs. "Let's come into the living room and call that friend of yours."

"What's he doing?" I say, my eyes back on the staircase.

"A preliminary search. Just to see if there's anything out of the ordinary."

"Claire wasn't taken from home."

"Right now, it's hard to say what we're up against. It could be a wrong place, wrong time sort of thing. Or her abduction could have been premeditated. It's standard practice to look around the home."

"They don't know anything about us or our lives. How are they supposed to know if something looks off?"

Sanchez clears her throat. "Have you noticed anything? Since you've been home?"

I walk back to the living room, which leads into the kitchen. The dishes are still in the sink from dinner last night. We'd had meatloaf with mac and cheese. A shriveled-up banana sits on the table, where Claire forgot to put it in the bin. We were in a hurry this morning, trying to make sure we arrived at school in time for the field trip.

By the door, my laptop bag sits on a dresser; I left it home today. Beside it, is Claire's gymnastics bag. Everything looks so ordinary and normal, it hurts. I wish there was something out of place, a smoking gun that would lead me in the right direction. The only thing missing is my daughter.

"No. I haven't noticed anything."

I seem to drift into the living room. Before I know it, I'm sitting on the sofa, my head leaned back, so I can stare at the beige popcorn ceiling. Another project David and I had vowed to complete.

"Do you think it's premediated?" I ask.

"We don't know enough yet." Sanchez sits beside me. "Right now, it appears she was snatched while everyone was distracted."

"What does that mean? A stranger abduction."

"Most kidnappings are related to custody issues. But you said you don't have any ongoing issues?"

"None. The only family we have is my late husband's brother, and we rarely speak." I sit up straighter, aware that Sanchez is avoiding my original question. "If it is a stranger abduction, what does that mean?"

Her jaw is tense, her lips closed. Then, "It means the next twenty-four hours are crucial. So, we need to investigate as much as possible as quickly as possible."

She doesn't want to tell me, but it doesn't matter, because I already know. Most often, when a child is taken by a stranger, it's for a sinister purpose. The types of evil and depravity I can't even imagine, especially now, with my daughter gone. If we don't get her back soon—if there's not an innocent explanation—she might never come home.

"I can't lose Claire," I say, my voice cracking. "She's all I have left."

Sanchez pats my arm. "How about we give that friend a call?"

TWENTY

More cops arrive. Some in uniforms, some in plain clothes. The underdressed ones make themselves comfortable at the kitchen table, opening laptops and plugging in other devices.

"What are they doing?" I ask Sanchez.

"Setting up equipment," she says, her eyes never leaving her phone. "We'd like to search your computer, too. In case Claire made contact with anyone online."

"She's six. She barely knows how to use a computer."

"You'd be surprised."

Without saying anything else, I walk to the front door and retrieve my laptop, which she gives to another officer. I have nothing to hide. If there's anything on our computer, in this house, on my phone that will help bring home Claire, they're welcome to it.

"Let me in." The voice at the door is Sarah. A young female officer is stopping her from coming inside. "She called me."

"She's fine," Sanchez says. Everyone is taking direct orders from her, it appears. The female officer lowers her hand, and Sarah storms inside.

"I still can't believe it," she says, wrapping her arms around me. I can feel her own heart beating against my chest, her adrenaline spiking. "I don't even know what to say."

"I think it was a mistake leaving the pumpkin patch," I tell her. "What if she's still there? She could be hiding in the cornfields, like Katy."

"There were a ton of people searching the property when I left. They'll find her," Sarah says. "It's already on the news. Everyone will be looking for her."

My mind conjures the scene from earlier, everyone searching frantically for Katy. The unease I felt then returns and expands, despair setting in.

"Someone could be hiding her. She could have been... kidnapped." I struggle to say the last word. "The whole place was on lockdown while we were searching for Katy, but after we found her, people left all at once. There's no telling who could have her. It was so chaotic."

"Exactly. It's possible she got turned around. Try to stay positive and not jump to the worst scenario."

I want to believe her, but something inside is telling me that's not true. If this were a mistake, an accident, it would have been corrected by now. I fear the worst scenario is exactly what we're dealing with.

"Detective Sanchez?"

A plain-clothed policeman stands in the kitchen, waiting for Sanchez to re-enter the house. He's holding out his phone for her to see. Whatever she's watching, it surprises her. She looks over at me, only briefly, before turning her back, whispering something.

My pulse quickens. They've found her. Worse, they've found her body. Sarah can sense me tensing beside her. She squeezes my hand, a silent offering. When Sanchez walks back into the living room, it's as though her movements are in slow motion.

"There's something you need to see."

"Is it her?" I'm rocking back and forth now. "Is she alive?"

"We've not found her. But this could give us an idea of what's happening here." She turns her phone around so that Sarah and I can see. "This is security footage from McCallister's parking lot. It was taken about ninety minutes ago, around the time we released everyone. I need you to tell me if you recognize anyone in the video."

It's clear from the screen that the camera is angled high above the parking lot. Because everyone is walking toward their cars, it only shows people from behind. The video is zoomed in on an adult and a little girl. Neither of them turns around, so I can't see their faces, and both are nondescript.

"Let me play it again," Sanchez says.

Now the video is zoomed in more, playing on a loop. The footage is so blurry, I can't even tell if the adult is a man or a woman, let alone who he or she might be. There's nothing extraordinary about the little girl, either; she's wearing the same burnt-orange shirt as every other child on the field trip. As much as I wish I could identify my own child at first glance, the low-quality footage and awkward camera angle makes that hard.

I continue staring at the image, trying to make sense of it. Notice a small detail that will let me know whether it's her.

Then I see it.

The bright-pink ribbon tied around the girl's ponytail. Noticing that detail brings everything into focus. The profile of her face, even her walk.

The child in the video is Claire.

"It's her. I can tell by her bow," I say. "That's Claire."

The sight of her fills me with relief; at least I've been able to see her again. Then, the fear clutches tighter.

"What about the adult?" Sanchez asks. "Do you recognize them?"

Average height and build, wearing a hoodie with the hood

up. Those are the only details that register. Is he or she deliber-ately hunched over so the camera can't see? They have one arm extended, holding Claire's hand.

"I don't know."

"Are you sure?"

"Can *you* tell who that is?" Sarah asks Sanchez, defensively.

The detective ignores her. "If you're sure that's Claire in the video, and you don't know who the adult is, then we can assume she's not lost. She's been abducted."

The video continues playing on a loop, and I can't peel my eyes away. I stare at Claire, hoping this isn't the last image I'll ever have of her, then I look at the person leading her into the parking lot, gripped with fear and outrage that I don't know who it is.

TWENTY-ONE

The video confirms that we're dealing with the worst possible scenario. Deep down, I think I knew this is what had happened, even if I didn't want to admit it.

"Why would someone take her?" I'm sitting on the sofa, my feet pulled up.

"When we're dealing with a stranger abduction, there's two scenarios. This could be a ransom attempt. If the person who took Claire has no connection to you or her, it could mean we should be expecting demands soon."

"Ransom? We don't have any money. Why would someone choose us?"

"Maybe they didn't. Maybe they just saw an opportunity to snatch a random child, and they're waiting to get their ducks in a row before they make contact."

"What's the other reason?" I ask.

Sanchez exhales. "This person wants to harm Claire."

Hearing my worst fears spoken aloud makes me gasp. "No!"

"I know how difficult that must be to hear, but it's something we need to prepare ourselves for. If that's what's happened, then we must work even faster to follow any clues that might lead us to Claire."

Sarah has sat silently, listening. She stands now, shakily, her eyes on the floor. "I'm going outside. I need some air."

All she's done since arriving at the house is comfort me, but it appears the possibility that we might have already lost Claire is too much to bear. I too know the statistics, even if I don't want to believe them. A child that's taken by a predator is usually dead within twenty-four hours. If that's what's happened here, Claire's time might have already run out.

I start breathing fast and heavy, leaning forward to keep the spins at bay. I'm tempted to grab the anxiety medication in my purse, but I don't need my mind to be hazy right now. I need to think clearly.

Sanchez places her hand on my back. "Hold it together, Emma. Your daughter needs you."

"There's nothing I can do," I cry. "I'm here and she's... no one knows where she is. Who she's with. How am I supposed to help her?"

"I want you to watch the video again," she says. "Maybe there's a detail about the suspect you'll notice."

"I already told you; I can't make out anything."

She holds out the phone and I take it. The video plays again on a loop. "What about Claire? Is there anything you notice about her?"

"She looks calm. She doesn't look scared."

"Is she a trusting child?"

"Sure, but she wouldn't leave with a stranger."

"But the person in the video doesn't strike you as someone you know. Is it possible she'd leave with someone if she was manipulated in some way? Offered a toy or treat?"

"She knows not to do that."

But I wonder. I know how the mind of a kindergartener works; I'm surrounded by more than a dozen of them each day.

They might nod along when we preach to them about stranger danger, but when put to the test, the idea of free candy or a cute pet overwhelms their logic. They're children, after all. If a stranger walked up to Claire and offered to give her something, would she take the bait?

"Is there anyone from school that makes you uneasy?"

"Uneasy?"

"We're women. And mothers. We all know the feeling of someone that gives us the creeps. Stares a little too long. Has a way of being places they shouldn't."

"I can't think of anyone like that."

"How about at any of Claire's sports practices or extracurriculars?"

"No! There's no one who would do something like this, okay?" I shout, standing and walking across the room. I lean against the bureau, trying to stabilize my breath. "I'm sorry. I know you're only trying to help, but if I had even an inkling, I'd let you know."

"No one thinks they know someone who would do this sort of thing," she says, plainly. "And yet it still happens. More than we'd like to admit."

She's right. There's no way of understanding how truly depraved another person can be, but all I know is that today started out like any other day in our lives. A normal day.

And now we're here, overwhelmed with more heartache than I could even imagine.

TWENTY-TWO

My thoughts are interrupted by a blaring alarm. It's coming from my phone. As I race to retrieve it, I realize it's not only my phone making a noise. Every phone in the room is.

"What's going on?" I ask.

"Now that we're certain she's been abducted, we've issued an AMBER alert," Sanchez says.

The alarms blare together, like a symphony, as people rush to silence them. I've received countless messages like this over the years, when another local child is missing. Usually, they're returned safely. Or so I assume. Now that I think about it, I don't know I've ever taken the time to get online and check the outcome.

Instead, I read the details about the missing person, making a mental note to say something if I see something. But no one ever really sees anything useful, do they? Those alerts are forgotten in the time it takes for another notification to come in.

I read the information that's been sent out:

Claire.
Six years old.

Blonde hair. Blue eyes.
Wearing an orange shirt and black leggings.
Last seen leaving McCallister's Pumpkin Patch with
unknown adult.

There's a phone number to call with information, and a link leading to more details.

When I click the link, the school picture I sent to Sanchez fills the screen. It's odd to think my daughter's image has been sent to this many people in a matter of seconds.

"I need some air too," I say, as I walk outside.

It's starting to rain. A soft drizzle alongside the approaching nightfall.

I used to enjoy rainy evenings. It was a calm permission to cancel my plans, hunker down for the night with David or Claire.

When I step outside tonight and feel the gentle pecks of raindrops on my cheek, I want to cry. Claire is out there alone. Does she have shelter? Is she dry? Has she eaten anything? Soon, night will set in. She's never spent a night away from me.

I circle around to the back of the house, looking for Sarah.

When I find her, she's standing on the back porch. In one hand, she's holding her phone up to her ear. In her other hand, she holds a cigarette. The smoke hovers around her, caught in the humid air.

Her end of the conversation carries, her voice frustrated.

"This isn't the time to talk... I don't care about that." A pause, as I watch her take a hit off the cigarette. "She needs me right now. Don't you understand that?"

She moves to the left and catches sight of me. She quickly gets off the phone.

"Sorry about that," she says. "It won't happen again."

"Was that Darren?"

"Yeah. I was in the middle of watching the local news when he called."

"Since when did you start smoking again?"

"I always have an emergency stash in my car. It's a bad habit that's hard to break. Between Darren and this..." She takes another drag without looking at me. "Tonight calls for one."

"You said you were watching the news. Which station?" I ask.

She looks up now, stuffing her phone in her back pocket. She crosses her arms. "All the local channels have it."

I pull out my own phone, pecking letters into the search bar.

"Don't look," she says. "It will only make things worse."

"How could this possibly get any worse?"

I pull up a recent video posted by the same station that tried calling me a half hour ago. It's a three-minute clip. When it starts, the local anchor, Melanie McDaniel, is in the studio. She's wearing a lavender suit, her hair frizz-free and pulled away from her face.

"Breaking tonight," she begins, staring directly into the camera. "A six-year-old girl has been reported missing. It's believed the child went missing during a North Ridge Elementary school trip. Brian Mitchell is at the scene with more. Brian?"

The camera cuts to the reporter. He's standing near the entrance of McCallister's Pumpkin Patch, several police vehicles still on the scene. He's wearing a rain poncho, in preparation for the storm settling in.

"Thank you, Melanie. The call came in just before four o'clock this afternoon. Six-year-old Claire was reported missing, last seen here at McCallister's Pumpkin Patch, where she was attending a field trip with her kindergarten class.

"I'm told police were already on the scene for an unrelated incident, but their quick response has done little in helping find Claire. She has blonde hair and blue eyes. She was last seen wearing an orange North Ridge Elementary shirt. If you have any information, you should call the number at the bottom of the screen."

Brian is replaced with the same photo of Claire they issued with the AMBER alert. Her snaggle-tooth smile breaks something inside me. I rub my thumb against the picture, wishing I could just as easily reach out and touch her. My daughter is all I have left, and I'm no closer to finding her.

"Are you okay?" Sarah asks. I'd forgotten she was standing beside me.

Before I can answer, Melanie McDaniel starts talking again.

"Brian, is there anything you can tell us about how the child went missing?"

"Again, she was at the pumpkin patch for a field trip. Both parents and school staff were present. It appears the mother had left her daughter in the care of someone else when she was taken."

"What?" I shout back, knowing I won't get a response. "Why would they say that?"

Sarah exhales slowly, a knowing look on her face. Was this the part she didn't want me to see?

"There isn't much they can report," she says. "They're just looking for something to fill the airtime."

"Are they suggesting I'm at fault?" I ask. Sarah shrugs, helplessly. "That's not what happened. I was busy looking for Katy. I was a teacher doing my job. Why won't they report that? I wasn't neglecting my child."

A guilty thought creeps in. Yes, I was doing my job. I was trying to protect a student, and in that moment, my own daughter was taken. Maybe I made the wrong choice. I should have watched my own daughter, instead of falling victim to the familiar tug-of-war that is being both a parent and a professional.

I shut off my phone, unwilling to hear the rest of the report.

I sit on the concrete steps, dropping my head into my hands. Raindrops are falling more heavily, darkening the gray stone beneath my feet, a reminder that time is passing, life is continuing, and I still have no idea where my daughter is.

"I can't do this," I say. "I can't stand not knowing what happened. Who has her? Who was that person in the parking lot? Why isn't the news sharing that?"

Sarah sits beside me, rubbing my shoulders. "Maybe they don't have the video yet. Or maybe they're waiting to release it."

"That's what they should be talking about. Not me. They could release the video. Someone might recognize them. Someone who is willing to help."

But even as I speak the suggestion aloud, I feel helpless. I've watched the video enough times to know there isn't a clear image of the kidnapper's face, but there could be something in that video that captures someone's attention, like Claire's pink hair ribbon did for me. Something in the way the person walks, something about the clothing.

"Is there anything I can do for you?" Sarah asks. "Someone I can call? I feel useless just sitting around here."

"There's no one else."

"What about David's brother and his wife? Don't they live near here?"

"We're not close, you know that. There's nothing they can do."

"Still, it's family. It might be good for you—"

"I've been avoiding them since David died. I'm not going to reach out now. Besides, they're always traveling. Last time I checked in, they'd just returned from Greece."

"Claire is their niece. I'm sure they're willing to do anything to help find her."

"But there's nothing they can do!" I shout, standing now. "I don't need David's rich brother and his trophy wife walking around the house, watching my every move. It's bad enough the news stations are labeling me a bad mom."

"They're not saying that—"

"Aren't they? *The mother left her daughter in the care of someone else.* I'm the bad guy here, don't you get it? It's always the mother's fault."

"I was the one you left her with," Sarah says, with tears in her eyes. "If anyone is at fault, it's me."

It's a complicated feeling. Yes, Sarah was with her, but what happened could have just as easily happened to me or anyone else. I think of Laura and the way she was beating herself up. No wonder Sarah is out here chain-smoking. Her own guilt must be eating her alive.

"I don't blame you. If someone was there with the intention of snatching a child, all the children were in danger. If it wasn't Claire, it would have been someone else."

"I wish it had been another child," she looks away. "I know it's awful to say that, but it's true."

I don't know how to respond, because I relate to what she's saying. As much as I wish no child was in danger, I wish even more Claire was with us now.

"Ms. Howard?" It's one of the uniformed police officers. "Detective Sanchez needs you."

"What is it?" I ask, already walking toward him. "Have they found something?"

"We've received a phone call from someone claiming they have Claire."

TWENTY-THREE

I'm not very wet, and yet as I stand in the living room, waiting for Sanchez's instructions, I'm shivering. Sarah notices, wraps a blanket around my shoulders.

"What did they say?"

"It was a dropped call," Sanchez says. "They called the landline. Claimed they had taken Claire and said they'd be calling back in five minutes with instructions."

"Was it a man, a woman?" Sarah butts in.

"The voice was distorted using one of those apps," she answers. "This could be a good thing. If the kidnapper is after money, there's no reason for them to hurt Claire."

"But I don't have money! I'm struggling month-to-month as it is. Surely, whoever took her would know that."

"Only if the abduction was premeditated. If she was taken out of convenience, the kidnapper may not know how much you're worth. Besides, don't worry about the amount. We can negotiate. Keep them talking, give us more time to find Claire."

Negotiate? As though my daughter's safety is up for debate, like a good car deal or an ideal mortgage rate. I'm not trying to counter their offer. I'm willing to give them whatever they want, if it means bringing my daughter home safely.

Sanchez holds out her wrist, looking at her watch. "It's almost time. We need to clear the room."

Several officers start walking to the front door. Sarah stands.

"I'll be waiting outside. If you need anything, let me know."

Now there are only a handful of detectives left. Three of them are sitting at the dining room table, fiddling with laptops and wires. Sanchez sits in front of me, the look on her face intense.

"You want to keep them on the phone. The longer they're on the line, the easier it will be for us to track. It's not like the movies, where we can get an exact location in a matter of seconds."

"What do I say?"

"Keep talking about Claire. You want to say her name as much as possible. Humanize her. Ask if she's okay. Say you want to speak with her. The story is all over the news, so the caller must already know police are involved. Don't worry about that. Keep the focus on your daughter, keeping her safe. Listen to the demands but keep bringing up Claire."

"What if they ask for money?"

"Don't commit to anything. Just keep—"

The phone rings.

TWENTY-FOUR

Silence, until a second ring trills. My heart feels caught in my throat. I'm scared to move, scared to do anything.

"Wait," shouts one of the men at the dining room table. One of his hands is glued to the keyboard. "Don't answer until the fourth ring."

Another ring. I look at Sanchez, eyes wide.

"You can do this," she whispers. "Stay calm."

The fourth ring comes, and I answer.

"Hello?"

"Is this Emma Howard?" Just as Sanchez had said, the voice is distorted. Robotic and staticky, not human.

"Y-yes," I stammer, hating myself for not being braver.

"I have your daughter. She's alive."

"Is Claire hurt?" I ask, remembering the detective's commands. "Is Claire there? Can I speak to her?"

"We need twenty thousand dollars in cash."

"Cash?"

My eyes cut to Sanchez, a silent plea for help. The call is being broadcast to the entire room, so she knows what the caller is saying, but I'm frightened.

She mouths back to me, "Claire."

"Small bills, no tracking," the caller continues. "We want *you* to make the drop."

"I need to talk to Claire," I say, a subtle strength in my voice. "I need to know if she's okay."

"Take the money to the corner of Fillburn Street and Lucky Avenue. Leave it there. Avoid the highway and cut through the cornfields to make the drop," the voice continues. We're carrying on two completely different conversations. Just as I'm determined to get Claire back, the caller is determined to get the ransom. "No police. If we're being followed or traced, the deal's off. Got that?"

"Yes."

"Repeat it back to me."

I bring my palm to my head, trying to remember. "Twenty thousand dollars. Fillburn and Lucky. No police."

"Good. You're only going to have one shot at this, Emma, so make sure you get it right."

"What about Claire? Will she be there?"

"Follow the instructions and you'll get your daughter back."

I sense the caller is getting ready to disconnect, and I'm desperate for my own demands to be heard.

"She's a sweet child. She doesn't like the dark or the rain. She hasn't done anything to deserve this. Please, please let me speak to her. I need to know she's okay."

"Make the drop at seven thirty. Not before or after."

"Please! Just let me speak to Claire. I need to know she's okay."

There's a split-second pause. No one speaks, but the line is still connected. Then, a scream. A little girl's scream, alive and uninhibited. My chest breaks open at the sound.

"Seven thirty, Emma."

The line goes dead.

TWENTY-FIVE

I hang up the phone and curse. It doesn't matter how hard I try, there's always something putting the plan at risk. But I have to play along, keep the game going a little bit longer, so that when I make my final move, no one will be watching.

I knew when I started this it wouldn't be simple. And I have a little bit of time to kill. I can't leave town until after eight o'clock anyway. I promised myself one more evening in this house, and that's a promise I plan to keep.

I scroll back through the messages on my phone, trying to ground myself, not spiral through thoughts of how this could all go wrong. The message about a missing child has been sent to everyone in the area. The thought of this message interrupting people as they sit down for dinner or settle in to watch television makes me smile. I created this. All this panic and confusion. In many ways, this is the most important thing I've ever done.

Curiosity gets the better of me, and I turn on the television. Sure enough, they're talking about the girl on there, too. Those reporters spew off facts like they're giving directions. Like if people only watch closely enough, it'll lead them to me. But that won't happen. I've made sure of it.

Now, they're talking about the mother, suggesting she might have something to do with it. I try not to think about her right now. Her pain may be real, but it's nothing compared to mine. If she truly cared about her daughter, she never would have let her out of her sight.

I check my phone. It's after six o'clock already. Now I have to leave the house, that doesn't leave me much time to pack.

It's a good thing I'm prepared. It only takes me two trips to get everything I need out of the shed and into the house. The rain is really starting to pick up. I lean the shovel against the wall. I take a long, hard look at the basement door, think of the girl sleeping just beside the steps.

It's going to be a long night.

For both of us.

TWENTY-SIX

EMMA

I fall back onto the sofa, fighting hard to catch my breath. The chilling sound of a child's scream rings in my ears.

"Did we get a location?" Sanchez shouts to the men at the table.

"It's local."

"Did we get a location?" she repeats.

"Not anything beyond the tower. The phone cut out before we could get any more than that."

Sanchez curses under her breath. She turns to me now, kneeling on the floor. "You did great."

"We don't know where they are. It didn't work."

"You made contact and heard their demands. That's what matters."

"That scream. Was it Claire? Do you think they hurt her?"

"They made it clear they're after money. That's good. They're not going to harm your daughter if they think that could stop them from getting the cash."

"But I don't have cash! Twenty thousand dollars? I couldn't come up with that kind of money in the next six months, let alone the next hour."

"Don't worry about that. We have other avenues we can take if you can't come up with the money—"

"Other avenues! Negotiations! This isn't a fucking treaty! This is my little girl!"

I stand quickly, pushing past Sanchez and marching toward the front door.

I didn't realize how hot I was feeling until the damp air hits my skin. The sky is getting darker, time continuing. I inhale and exhale in quick succession, trying to catch my breath. I lean forward, a dizzy spell threatening to send me falling.

"Emma, what happened?" Sarah says, running toward me. She steadies me, forcing me to sit on the porch steps.

"They have Claire. And they want money."

"That's good, right? It means they won't hurt her."

"If they don't get their money, they will. And I don't have twenty thousand dollars!"

Sarah sits beside me, defeated. The small window of hope has closed, and she too realizes how dire the situation is.

"If I don't meet their demands in the next ninety minutes, I'm never going to see my daughter again."

Sarah can't say anything. She looks down, and I wonder if she is trying not to cry in front of me.

"Emma?" Sanchez stands in the open doorway. "We need you back in here. We have to discuss our next move."

Our next move. Every half hour, it feels like we've entered a new round in a game, trying to stay ahead of our unidentified opponent. Strategize. Play a part. Remain calm.

But this is real, and what's at stake is Claire.

"So, what's our plan of action?" I ask, remaining on the front porch, my arms crossed over my chest.

"Our team is working several different angles," Sanchez says. "There's a chance we might be able to pull more from the video, or even the phone call. In the meantime, we need to prepare for what will happen if we go through with the ransom.

This is going to come out as rather blunt, but do you have access to the amount that was requested?"

I scoff. "I'm a single mother and a public-school teacher. I don't have the money." My gaze wanders to the front door. "I'm screwed."

"Let's not get too far ahead of ourselves," she says. "How much money could you access within the next hour? Cash."

"Five thousand. Maybe six."

When David died, we lost our insurance. That meant Claire and I had to take out a policy through the school, which cut into my income—the income that was now solely responsible for paying the mortgage and all our other bills. David and I both had measly life insurance policies we took out after Claire was born, but that sum covered little more than the funeral expenses. Neither of us thought we'd ever have to use them.

"If the kidnapper calls back, you might be able to ask for more time," Sarah says, trying to help. "Tell him you have some of the money but need to ensure Claire is safe before you give him the rest."

"There is no rest! And I'm not telling him there's no money. Then he has no reason to give Claire back."

She begins again. "If the kidnapper calls back—"

I cut her off. "He said he's not calling back. That this was our only communication."

"That's what he said, but these situations are fluid."

These situations. "This person has my daughter. I'm inclined to believe what he says. He said if I wanted to get Claire back safely, I had to have twenty thousand dollars. I don't have that."

"We're trying to stay positive," Sanchez says. "We're going to work with what we have to the best of our ability."

"But I don't have the money!"

I stomp back inside the house, Sarah and Sanchez following me. Two officers are standing in front of the living room television. The channel is stuck on a national news network, and they're talking about Claire.

"Is that *The Meghan Lachlan Show*?" I ask. "Have they picked up Claire's abduction?"

"Emma, try to focus," Sanchez says.

"No, I want to know what she's saying."

I've never been big about following the news. Usually, it's nothing but more reasons for me to be upset with the world. But everyone knows Meghan Lachlan. Her show is on a national news network, and the most scandalous clips are usually repeated throughout the day in little snippets on Instagram and Facebook. She covers an array of issues. It must have been a slow news day for her to pick up Claire's disappearance so quickly, and I'm not sure whether to be grateful the story is in front of such a wide audience, or nervous about what she's going to say.

"Tonight, we're hearing details about a young girl who was allegedly abducted from a school field trip. We're going to tell you everything we know so far, and, as always when discussing missing persons cases, make sure you pay attention." She pauses for poignancy. "It only takes one person."

That line has become Lachlan's catchphrase whenever she's reporting on crimes, followed by: *If you see something, give us a call.* She's known for reporting on salacious stories, and it unsettles me that Claire has now become one. I listen as she tells her viewers the same details that have been issued by the police.

"Why aren't they showing the video of the person with Claire at the pumpkin patch?" I ask Sanchez. I notice she too has been lured into the news program.

"We've been sending out information as we receive it, but it takes time. There are lots of boxes that have to be checked."

"But if they're asking for help finding her abductor, they need to know what they look like."

"You know as well as I do that it's hard to make out who that person is. As soon as the higher-ups release the video, my bet is they'll air it. It's been less than an hour since we sent it in, which seems like a long time to us, but isn't when we're talking about a police investigation."

"We're wasting too much time." My eyes are back on the screen, listening as Meghan Lachlan invites her guest anchor to make a comment.

"What are your thoughts on what we're seeing so far?" she asks.

"We have a school field trip. We have dozens of kids and even more adults in an isolated location," the man begins. "In my opinion, this is a case of too many cooks being in the kitchen. Everyone assumes the other person is watching a child when, in reality, no one is."

"What about reports that another student had been reported missing earlier in the day?"

"That student was located in a timely manner, but it's possible that incident created a window for someone to come in and snatch little Claire."

"We know the mother was on this trip as a chaperone. What does that tell you?"

"Well, we're aware most abductions do involve a close family member. It's a little hard to believe her daughter was taken right in front of her, and she didn't see anything."

They're twisting the chain of events. I wasn't a parent chaperone intentionally ignoring Claire. I was a teacher trying to find a missing student.

"Why are they doing this? They're acting as though I'm at fault."

"The media outlets we're contacting are spreading information as fast as they can. But when it comes to programs like Meghan Lachlan, it's about getting viewers, not facts. It's hard, but you should ignore it." Sanchez walks over to the television and turns it off. "Right now, we need to talk about the ransom drop."

"Why don't you tell *them* about the ransom?" I ask. "They can't say I'm involved if they know someone has already contacted us requesting money."

"Telling the media about the ransom request will do nothing but muddy the waters. It's important we keep some information close to the vest. We want to maintain leverage."

Claire is still missing, I'm not even close to having enough money to cover the ransom demands and, thanks to Meghan Lachlan, the entire country will soon suspect I did something to harm my own daughter. I don't believe that leaves me with much leverage at all.

TWENTY-SEVEN

Sanchez remains quiet, giving my nerves a moment to settle.

"I'm going to catch up with the officers outside. Try to stay calm and clear your head," she tells me. "You'll need to stay focused for the ransom drop."

But my mind is anything but focused. If I'm not thinking about Claire, my mind is back on *The Meghan Lachlan Show*, wondering what she's saying about me.

"You look awful, Emma," Sarah says. "Can I get you something to eat? Something to drink?"

"No. I just need a moment to myself. I need to figure out what I'm going to do."

I sneak onto the back porch, phone in hand, and search for the most recent video on *The Meghan Lachlan Show* website.

As expected, Lachlan is continuing to discuss Claire, and I'm compelled to listen.

I shouldn't care what they're saying about me, and yet, hearing anyone talk about Claire right now, even if I'm being portrayed as a villain, makes me feel closer to her. It's proof that she exists in the world, that she matters.

Still, when I see Meghan Lachlan's face, my stomach

turns. With little evidence, the woman has already insinuated that I've done something to harm Claire. It's a salacious story, one other parents have unfortunately made a plausible scenario, but it doesn't apply to me. I would never hurt my daughter.

"We've been able to obtain video from when Claire went missing," Meghan announces. "We ask our viewers to watch closely, in case they notice something or someone. Remember, it only takes one person."

I hope Claire's abduction video being shared on live television will capture someone's attention. As much as I hate to give credence to anything Meghan Lachlan says, it does only take one person to recognize something familiar. To me it is a stranger, could be anyone. But to someone else, it could be a son, a sister, a friend.

And yet, the video that appears on the screen is not of Claire leaving the pumpkin patch. It looks to be a video taken from a cell phone, likely by one of the parents.

"This was submitted by someone at the scene," the guest anchor explains, as the video plays. "It really gives a sense of the chaos that was taking place when the girl was taken."

The camera scans the children playing on the playground, but I'm not able to spot Claire, or recognize any child from that distance. The video pans back and forth, showing the parents lining up at the gate, waiting for information and begging to get in.

"Why has such a large crowd formed?" Meghan asks.

"It's my understanding that the people you see lined up on the other side of the gate arrived once word got out that the first child was missing."

"Two children missing from the same location."

"The first child wandered off from the group and was found," he says. "I'm told that during this time parents attending the field trip were told to stay on the property. They had already been given permission to leave before anyone realized little Claire was missing."

"Is it possible one of the parents in this video took Claire?"

"Yes. From what I understand, the pumpkin patch ended their lockdown a mere ten minutes after this video was taken. Take a close look at all the faces in the crowd. Claire's abductor could be right in front of us."

But I'm not looking at the crowd. My gaze has landed on something else, in the very corner of the screen. As the camera goes back and forth, it captures a glimpse of someone standing beside the ticket booth, on the far side of the building.

I race back into the house.

"Sarah, is that you? In the corner of the video?"

I find her in the kitchen, drinking a glass of water. She seems startled by the tone in my voice. She takes my phone and looks at the clip.

"I... uh, yeah. I think it is."

"You're smoking."

Her eyes go wide. "I told you the stress has been getting to me."

"But we were on the field trip. Smoking isn't allowed anywhere on the property."

"I didn't think I'd be caught. And I certainly didn't think the tape would end up on the news."

"When was this video taken? You were with me the entire day. Up until Katy went missing."

"I snuck one in. That's it."

"But when?"

Her cheeks are turning red, the veins in her neck beginning to strain. "I don't know."

But the commentators on *The Meghan Lachlan Show* already said. This video was taken in the minutes before people were allowed to leave, which means it was taken during the time Sarah should have been watching Claire.

"Yes, you do. If you weren't with me and you weren't with Claire, then when was this?"

"There were adults everywhere. I just thought I'd sneak around the building long enough for a few puffs. I couldn't have been gone more than two minutes. Three at most."

"You left Claire to do that?"

"When I got back, half of our group had crawled into the tunnels. I thought Claire was with them."

"That's how Claire went missing. Because you took your eyes off her."

"It was just for a minute. I started looking for her the moment I got back, and when I couldn't find her, that's when I started asking others to help."

"But you never told me you left her. You said you were with her the entire time."

"I was. Except for those couple of minutes."

"What's going on here?" Sanchez asks.

"Sarah wasn't with Claire when she was taken," I say. "She'd snuck off to have a cigarette."

"I'm sorry!" Sarah is crying now.

"Is this true?" Sanchez asks.

"It was only for a second. When I came back, I assumed she was with the other kids."

"You should have told us this from the beginning."

"I know, but I..." She stops and looks at me. "I didn't think you'd ever forgive me."

I'm not sure I ever will. Sarah has been one of my closest friends, at school and otherwise. She was there for me in the wake of David's death. While I was continuing to push others away, I let her in. I never thought she'd take her eyes off my daughter, and I never thought she would lie to me about it.

"We're going to need you to come down to the station and give a new statement. We need to make sure you're not leaving anything else out."

But Sarah isn't listening to Sanchez. She's only focusing on me. "I'm so sorry, Emma. Please. Say something."

"Just go."

I walk away, the news feed from *The Meghan Lachlan Show* still playing on my phone.

It only takes one person.

Yes, it only takes one person's insight to find a missing child.

And it only takes one person's mistake to put one in danger.

TWENTY-EIGHT

I'm getting warmer, my skin beginning to itch. I'm boiling over with anger. At Sarah. At Meghan Lachlan. At the mystery person who took my daughter.

All these problems are spiraling before me, and there's nothing I can do to fix them.

"Are you okay?" Sanchez is back in the room.

"No, I'm not. Sarah was the only person I trusted to help me get through this. Now I know she's a liar. And not just about smoking the cigarette. We don't know anything about what was really happening when Claire was taken!"

I think about Laura's reaction to losing Katy at the pumpkin patch, not being completely truthful about how long she'd been missing. It's human nature to want to protect yourself when you fear you're at fault. Or maybe it's simpler than that. Perhaps Laura really did think Katy had only been gone a few minutes.

But Sarah's lie feels more intentional. Claire is missing, and every detail about her disappearance could help find her. Sarah saw the video of the person leaving the pumpkin patch with Claire. I told her about the ransom demands. And she still deliberately held back information.

"Sarah is on her way to the police station," Sanchez says. "If she has any useful information, we'll get it out of her."

"You don't sound confident?"

"I'm confident about my colleagues," she says. "But I doubt Sarah has more information. Lying about the smoking? That was just to protect herself. Self-preservation. As a mother, and a friend, I understand your anger toward her. But I don't know how much this changes what happened."

What it changes is my friendship with Sarah, and my ability to trust anyone. Ever since David died, I've tasked myself with handling everything on my own, and it's precisely because of situations like this. The moment I give the reins over to someone else, the entire ride goes off the tracks.

"Why aren't you questioning her?" I ask. "I thought you were the lead investigator."

"Right now, my focus is preparing you for the ransom drop. A conversation with Sarah will have to wait."

"Sanchez," an officer at the front door interrupts. "We have some people out front requesting to come in. They say they're family."

The detective looks at me, her forehead wrinkling. "I thought you didn't have any family?"

"We don't."

"What are their names?" the detective asks the officer.

"Steven and Piper Howard."

Sanchez looks back at me. "Ring a bell?"

"Yeah," I say, turning my back to the door. I release a slow, long exhale. "That's my husband's brother and my sister-in-law."

David's family. They used to be mine. Or at least, Steven did. He didn't marry Piper until after David died. I've met her a couple of times, but I can't say I really know her. And I'm wondering why they've decided to come here. We aren't close. They must have received the AMBER alert, like everyone else.

Steven walks into the room first, looking so much like David my heart almost stops. They look very much alike. Both tall, with dark hair, olive skin. Even their eyes look the same, which is one of the reasons I avoid looking at Steven for too long. He's wearing a dark trench coat.

Piper is behind him, shaking the rain off an umbrella. My sister-in-law fits the trophy wife stereotype to a tee. Piper is in her mid-twenties with blonde hair that's effortlessly undone. She teaches Pilates at a studio downtown, when she isn't gallivanting around the globe with her older, wealthier husband.

When Steven sees me, he storms past the officers at the front door and almost knocks me over with a hug.

"My God, Emma. Why didn't you call?" He doesn't sound angry, but worried. Scared. When I try to pull away, I realize he's still clinging to me, afraid to let go. "Not Claire. We can't lose her, too."

I force myself away, feeling the damp on my clothes from where he's been outside. The storm must be getting stronger. Piper tries to reach out to me, but I hold up my hands.

"Sorry, I just need some space."

"I understand," she says, sitting on the sofa. Her eyes scan the room, landing nowhere. "I can't even imagine what you're going through. How worried you must be. I'm just happy we can help."

"Help?"

"The money," Steven says. "We brought cash."

How did they know to bring cash? How did they know about the ransom at all? Even the news stations haven't picked it up, as far as I know. All Meghan Lachlan seems to be reporting is my possible involvement.

"I never asked you to bring money," I say. "How did you even know about the ransom?"

"Your friend called us," he says. "Sarah."

In how many ways can Sarah mess this up for me? First, she

loses sight of my daughter. She lies about what she was doing at the time. Now, she's reaching out to estranged family members, something I explicitly told her I didn't want to do.

Steven and Piper made it big a few years back by investing in a start-up, some navigational tool called Voyage. The product blew up, giving them a whopping return on their investment. Now Steven barely works, other than playing the stocks, and Piper is a housewife when she's not at the Pilates studio. They don't have children, so they usually spend their time traveling.

"Let me get this right," Sanchez says. "You have the money to meet the ransom demands on hand?"

Steven responds by holding up a black duffel bag.

"Can I talk to you for a minute?" I ask Sanchez, pulling her away from the couple. I don't speak again until we're around the corner. "I didn't reach out to them. I didn't ask them to get involved."

"Why not? Is there something I should know?"

The history is complicated. Six months after David died, Steven invited us over to meet his new fiancée. We met one other time for a quick lunch, about a year later. We've had limited contact since then. I even avoided their wedding—a beachfront ceremony on the shores of Waikiki. Even when he offered to pay our way, I turned him down. Claire and I have struggled in the wake of David's death, and being around Steven, and now Piper, only makes it worse.

"We aren't close. We haven't been since my husband died. I didn't even reach out to them when Claire went missing."

"But why? You should be reaching out to as many people as possible."

"Steven isn't the kind of person you can depend on. He showed up drunk to his own brother's funeral. Before that, there were problems."

My words trail away, my mind conjuring memories from the night of the accident. The argument between the two brothers. The real reason I haven't been able to look Steven in the eye ever since that night. I push the thoughts away, focusing back on Sanchez.

"It doesn't seem right taking their money."

"What other option do you have?" She pauses. "This isn't the time for pride. You should be willing to do whatever it takes to get Claire back."

"Of course I'm willing to do whatever it takes!"

"Then get in there and make nice with your in-laws," she says. "You can be mad about this later. After we bring Claire home."

She's right, and I know it. For a moment, I'm ashamed I didn't consider it myself. I let the complications that have arisen in the wake of David's death cloud my judgement. Nothing should matter right now but finding Claire... I must remember that.

When I walk back into the living room, Steven and Piper are in conversation with another officer, hanging on her every word.

"You have the kidnapper on video?" Steven asks.

"Yes, but we haven't been able to make an identification," the officer says.

"Maybe we can take a look," Piper says. "See if there is something we recognize."

"Why would you recognize anything?" I ask, the words escaping before I can keep them still. "I was right there, and nothing stood out to me."

Piper averts her eyes. "I'm just thinking out loud. I don't know what else to do. I feel so helpless."

"The good news is, now that we have the cash, it should make the ransom drop seamless," Sanchez says. "The kidnapper gets their money, and we get Claire back."

"Could it really be that easy?" I ask.

"Maybe. Most kidnapping stories are only told when something goes wrong. Usually, if the kidnapper gets what he or she wants, there is reason to hurt the child."

But that doesn't mean Claire is safe. My mind returns to the Lindbergh case, that lone ladder that sparked countless conspiracies over the years. If this person is willing to kidnap a child, I doubt he or she knows how to care for one. She could still get hurt. She might already be suffering.

"Let's talk about how we want to do this," Sanchez continues. "Now, I know the caller said you should do the drop. Normally, we'd use a decoy. A female officer about your size and weight that could drop off the money."

"The caller said no police. The last thing I want to do is make this person angry."

"You have to think about your safety too," Sanchez says.

"I don't care about my safety!" I say. "I only want Claire back."

"Maybe you should listen to what they have to say," Steven says, with that condescending tone I imagine he uses in all his corporate meetings. "They're the experts."

"What, because you've come in here with a bag full of cash you think you get to call the shots now?"

"I wasn't saying that—"

"The caller said for *me* to do the drop," I continue. "That's what's happening."

Silence blankets the room. No one wants to look in my direction, challenge my position.

When someone breaks the trance, it's Sanchez.

"All right," she says. "Let's start prepping."

TWENTY-NINE

Thirty minutes. That's how long until we can make the drop.

The destination the caller sent over is only a ten-minute drive from my house. Sanchez has already sent officers to man the surrounding area, discreetly, of course. She doesn't want me to leave any sooner than necessary. She's hoping that whoever is watching, *if* someone is watching, they will be focused on me, not the police on the periphery.

And she doesn't want to offer up any extra time that could put me in danger.

So, I've moved to the back of the house, to the small den situated beneath the staircase. When David and I first moved in, we didn't know what to make of this room. It wasn't big enough to be a bedroom, but it was too large for storage. After a few months, we decided to turn the space into a music room. Even though David didn't have the time to play like he did when he was younger, he kept all his instruments and enjoyed playing for us when he could. Finally, David had a dedicated area for his music. And he thought it would be the perfect place to give Claire lessons when she was older.

The instruments hang on the wall still, collecting dust. I rarely go into this room anymore, but every other corner of the house has been invaded by strangers in police uniforms, it seems. So here I am, wandering around the room, staring at my dead husband's most-prized possessions, wishing I could remember the significance of each one.

"Steven still plays, you know." I'm startled. I turn to see Piper. She walks into the room without invitation, sitting on the narrow futon against the back wall. "In fact, he's even thinking about starting up a band. Can you believe that? He invites his buddies over on the weekends. The music room at our house is always a mess."

I've been to their house. Their music room is the size of most people's basements. There's even a baby grand piano, a trophy piece because neither of them plays. I asked.

"I try to avoid this room."

"What about Claire? I'd think she'd get a kick out of seeing her dad's old things."

"I keep her out, too. Don't want to risk her breaking anything."

There's a pause, which stretches. I'm not sure which subject ushered in the awkwardness. David. Claire. The fact I try to keep her away from her father's things.

There's always been a barrier between myself and Piper, and even though it would be easy to blame it on my unresolved issues with Steven, I believe the truth lies in the fact we have so little in common. She's almost ten years younger than me. She doesn't have a full-time job. She's not a mother and has no desire to become one. She looks more like an internet influencer who should be giving a hair tutorial on Instagram than someone I could share drinks with.

The first time I met her, she had already moved into Steven's mansion across town, a sparkling new diamond on her finger. There was a superficial edge to her that was hard to shake. Even the story of how they met seemed like a scene from a movie. She'd slipped on the steps of City Hall, on the same day Steven was there to file some paperwork for one of his businesses. He helped her to her feet, and then treated her to lunch. A week later, he was booking plane tickets for them to go on a vacation. Within two months, they were engaged. All this coming from a man whose idea of commitment was a three-date streak. Unbelievable. Situations like that didn't happen in real life. No, the real world was built for tragedy. Husbands who die in car accidents, children who go missing. At least that's the world I've known.

I often wonder what David would have thought of Piper, or about Steven settling down in general. Even though Steven is two years older, David was always the responsible one. They often fought about Steven's childishness, his choices. Getting rich only made Steven more stubborn because it convinced him he was living life the right way. And maybe he was, for him. But for people like David and myself, Steven's lifestyle was always out of touch. To see him now, a one-woman man with thriving businesses, I'm not sure how David would react. Would he be proud of his brother? Relieved? Jealous?

"Once we get Claire back," Piper says at last, "you should let Steven give her guitar lessons. I know he'd love that."

I spin around, a grimace on my face. "Don't do that. Don't come in here with your sing-song voice acting as though everything will be okay."

"I'm only trying to be positive—"

"And I'm being realistic. This is as bad as it gets."

"The ransom drop will get her back. I believe that."

"A lot could still go wrong. The last thing I need right now is someone giving me false hope."

She stands, walking over to me hesitantly. "Claire needs

you to be in her corner. She needs you to believe we'll get her back, no matter how far-fetched that might seem."

I exhale, finding it difficult to meet her eyes. "Look, I appreciate you and Steven stepping up with the ransom money. And when the time is right, I'll pay back every cent. I promise. But you're not a parent. I don't need your advice on how to react."

She turns, walking away. I think she is leaving the room, until she stops.

"Why didn't you call us sooner? We are your family, Emma. We should have heard Claire was missing from you, not the news or your friend."

"That friend is more family to me than either of you are." At least, she was.

"And whose fault is that? Steven and I... we've both tried to reach out to you in the past two years. We tried welcoming you both into our lives."

My gaze lands on one of David's favorite guitars. An acoustic. I can't remember the story behind it—where he bought it, or how much it cost. But I know on nights when we'd stay up late drinking and chatting, this is the one he'd pluck off the wall to serenade me. Sometimes singing my favorite songs, sometimes coming up with silly ones of his own.

Before I know it, I'm smiling, tears building in the corners of my eyes as I think about those lost memories and all the sorrow that has followed. I wipe my cheeks before turning to face Piper.

"Claire and I aren't collectibles. Life has been hard enough since David died. I shouldn't be burdened with what you and Steven are feeling, too."

Piper looks down. "I know it's been hard. But we're here to help. I only wish you could see that."

Is that the only reason they're here? To help? As Piper pointed out, I've avoided them at every turn for the past two years. She barely even knows Claire. And yet they arrive uninvited, asking questions about the investigation, all too eager to save the day.

There's a knock, and Sanchez peers inside the room.

"We're ready. Are you?"

"Yes," I say, brushing past Piper without saying another word.

THIRTY

The kidnapper was clear about where I'm supposed to go, and how I'm supposed to get there. Instead of taking the highway, which would be much faster, the directions insist I take a series of backroads leading to the corner of Filburn Street and Lucky Avenue. The farther away we are from civilization, the easier it will be for the kidnapper to tell whether I'm being tailed.

My car is the only one visible on the road, but Sanchez assured me the area is surrounded. Even now, alone in my car, I have her voice on speaker, guiding me.

"Are you turning on Filburn?" she asks.

"Yes."

"You're making good time. Our officers haven't spotted anything out of the ordinary just yet. Try to stay focused."

That's all I can do. My eyes land on the car radio. The meeting time is three minutes away. All I can hope is that in the next five minutes, this will be over, and Claire will be back in my arms.

"What do I do if no one is there?"

"Wait. They'll probably show up a few minutes later, just to cover their tracks." She pauses. "This is the last stoplight before we hit the backroads. Turn left on Gable."

"Left? I thought I was supposed to go right."

"That road has been closed for construction the past month. We're going to have to take the long way."

The long way.

My pulse hastens. I never turn left on Gable—haven't for more than two years. I never take this route because it leads right past where David crashed.

"Emma? You still with me."

"Yes." My voice is cracking. "Turning left on Gable."

"Hold it together," she warns. She's trying to keep me calm, and I appreciate that, but I didn't anticipate this drop becoming even harder. As my car makes its way down the road, moving closer to the cornfields in the distance, a newfound sense of dread takes over me.

I try not to think about where I am, rather focusing on what I'm doing. Getting Claire back. That's all that matters. It's not like this person intentionally sent me on this route. They just want a remote a spot as possible to make the exchange, so they can get the cash, and I can get my daughter back.

And yet this place has haunted me, in my thoughts and in my dreams. I've often wondered what David's final moments were like, out here on this abandoned stretch of road, the complete darkness of night surrounding him. What was it that made him run off the road in the first place? Some type of wild animal scurrying in front of his car? An imperfection in the rustic road that popped his tire? Or maybe it was the other person's fault.

What did he experience after the crash? Could he smell the sharp scent of gasoline? Did he hear the shattering glass? Did he feel any pain, or was he killed instantly, as the paramedics wanted me to believe?

No matter how hard I try to focus on Claire, on the importance of what I'm about to do, I can't shoo away these thoughts. These questions.

And then I see it. Up ahead of me, to the left. A duo of wooden crosses plunged into the dirt, bound together by a ribbon. I brake. It feels like I can't breathe, and yet I can't pull my eyes away from the crosses. I'm staring at the exact spot where my husband died.

"Emma, it looks like you stopped the car," Sanchez says. "What's going on?"

I can't answer her. In my mind, I'm hearing his voice singing, the melody of the guitar as he strums. I hear myself laughing. And I hear Claire giggling, calling for her father to play, "Louder, louder!"

I'm lost in the memories of our wedding day. Small and perfect, except for the rain, which continued to pour, much like it is right now. *Good luck*, our guests had said. *It's actually good luck to have rain on your wedding day.*

And I'm seeing the flash of red and blue lights that appeared outside our home. Remembering my anger that they would wake a sleeping Claire, too preoccupied to think further on what they could mean. Hearing the officer's voice as he climbed the front porch steps.

"I'm sorry, ma'am..."

Sanchez barks into the phone again. "Emma, what is going on?"

"I just need a minute."

"You can't do this now. We have a deadline."

Her voice echoes, my warring memories fighting for the forefront of my mind. I'm overcome with guilt. In my desperation to avoid my grief, I've pushed away everything about David. I wasn't even the one to leave this memorial. Perhaps it was Steven and Piper, the last of his family, who I refuse to see. All of these people have found a way to cope with David's loss, while all I can do is try, uselessly, to forget he ever existed.

"Emma, Claire needs you," Sanchez shouts.

I squeeze my eyes shut, feeling the tears stream down my cheeks. Eyes still closed, I put the car in drive and force myself to keep going, leaving the painful memories and the crosses in the dust behind me.

"We're moving again," Sanchez says to another officer. Then to me: "Are you good?"

"I can do this," I answer, repeating her words, "Claire needs me."

THIRTY-ONE

7:32

Sanchez tells me not to worry, that this is the kidnapper's way of showing me they are in control.

And it's working.

I feel completely helpless as I sit in my car, surrounded by the night fields, listening to the pattering of rain hit the hood, still shaken by the memories of David.

But Claire needs me. I have to remember that. Another minute passes.

"What if they don't show up?" I ask nervously.

"Give it time."

She sounds irritated, and it's hard to tell if she's irritated with me or just as anxious.

The rain falls harder, and I think again about my daughter, wondering if she's cold or dry. I wonder if she's as frightened as I am in this moment.

"There's a car coming," Sanchez says.

"I don't see any headlights."

"It's coming from the opposite direction. You should be seeing them in front of you in a matter of seconds."

Sure enough, a stream of light cuts through the tall cornstalks. I can tell the car is moving slowly, and another feeling of dread takes over.

"Should I get out of the car? Should I pull off the road?" The questions come fast. "Tell me what to do."

"Remain calm," she says. "Follow their lead."

The car creeps closer, and all I can think about is whether Claire is there with them. Finally, the car comes to a stall about ten feet ahead of me, on the other side of the road. The headlights flash.

Is that their way of telling me to exit the car? Are they confirming that it is me? I remain still, afraid of making a wrong move.

The driver's side door opens, and a man steps out. He's wearing something to cover his face, but it wouldn't matter. My own lights are beaming right at him, making it difficult to see. He shouts something.

I open my car door to hear him more clearly.

"Did you bring the money?" he says.

"Yes." I'm standing now. The bag with the cash rests beside me on the passenger seat.

"Take five steps forward and drop it on the ground."

Aside from our dueling headlights, it's so dark out here. I'm afraid to move away from the car, closer to the unknown, but I'm equally terrified of making the wrong move.

"Where is Claire?"

"Drop the money first," the man shouts. "Leave it on the ground, then walk back to your car. Slowly."

"Not until I see Claire!"

Sanchez told me to be compliant, follow his lead. We've made it this far. I'm not willing to keep going, to give this monster one more thing he wants, until I know my daughter is safe.

The man exhales, slamming the driver's side door shut.

I gasp, afraid he will march toward me. Instead, he walks toward the back of the car. He opens the trunk, reaching inside.

When he stands up, he's holding something. It looks like a sleeping child, from the way he cradles the bundle in his arms, but I can't see anything else. Her body is covered with a blanket. I wonder, is she sleeping? Or worse, is she injured? Dead?

"Drop the money first," he repeats. "Then walk back to your car, and I'll leave your daughter on the side of the road."

My chest bursts with hope. We're so very close. Without wasting another second to think, I lean into the car, grabbing the duffel bag. I step forward, dropping it on the ground.

The man pauses for a moment. He looks from left to right, assessing whether anyone else is nearby. He steps forward, still holding Claire in his hands, and scoots the bag closer to him with the heel of his boot.

"Give me Claire," I say, my pulse starting to spike. He has what he came here to get. He has the money. Why is he still holding my daughter?

He stands beside his vehicle, the bag at his feet. In one quick movement, he throws Claire to the ground, bending down in the same instant to grab the money.

THIRTY-TWO

I run toward her, shouting. The way he tossed her... the thud her body made when it hit the ground... something isn't right.

By the time I reach her, the man is already back in his car, speeding past me in the opposite direction. His tires kick up dirt, which dusts the inside of my mouth, lodges in my throat.

I begin to cough, fighting to get out her name.

"Claire! Are you okay? Are you hurt?"

There's no response. I try removing the blankets. With the light gone, it's impossible to see. But I keep feeling for her legs, for her arms, hoping for some small movement or sound.

There's nothing. She's still in my hands. Finally, I unravel the blankets where her face should be, and I feel for breathing. There isn't a nose or mouth. No face at all. What I'm feeling is some type of fabric, like burlap.

"Emma! Are you there? Tell me what's going on!"

The muffled sounds are coming from inside the car. Sanchez is shouting into the phone. I stand hurriedly, making my way back to the driver's seat. I grab my phone, still hearing Sanchez's voice, and shine the light on the bundle of blankets.

That's all it is. Blankets and burlap and other materials, woven together like a life-sized ragdoll.

No child.

No Claire.

"It isn't her," I say aloud.

"Emma? Is that you?"

I lift the phone to my ear. "It's not her. He didn't bring Claire."

"What about the ransom?"

"I gave him the money, and he took off."

"Don't move," she orders. "We'll be with you within two minutes."

But I'm only half-listening. This was supposed to be my chance to get my daughter back. All the strategizing and planning was for nothing.

THIRTY-THREE

I rush into the house. It was risky leaving her by herself, but I didn't have a choice. It's important I play along. Only a few more hours, and I'll be out of here for good. I won't have to worry anymore.

Besides, I don't think anyone followed me. I knew there were plenty of people around, whether they admitted it or not, but I was able to make a clean escape. I fish my cell phone out of my jacket pocket and turn it off. Once we're in the car, I'll toss it out a window. I can't allow for more distractions.

I hang my jacket by the door and shake the rain off my boots. I rush down the basement stairs to get a peek at her, make sure she's okay. She's still sound asleep. I spent weeks working on the right recipe. Something that would knock her out for a long time without harming her.

I head upstairs, leaving the girl alone in the dark.

For years, that's exactly how I felt, except no one was kind enough to put me to sleep. I spent all that time in darkness, and I remember every bit of it. There was nothing I could do. Until The Plan. After all this time, that's what saved me. I know it's a hard thing for people to understand.

All I ask is that those people imagine what I've been through. Only then, could they begin to appreciate how I got to where I am now.

The old grandfather clock in the living room begins to toll. Eight o'clock. It's time.

The problem with most people is they expect you to move past your pain, act as though it never happened. Dr. Meade understands that part of living with loss is about carving out time for remembrance.

For me, that time is at eight o'clock, every evening. I stop whatever I'm doing, light a candle, and pay tribute.

I remember her and I remember him. I take a few moments to imagine what our lives might have been like together. By giving myself these sacred minutes each day, it stops me from thinking about it all day long, diving into a world of make-believe that will never exist.

Now when I open my eyes, I think about the girl. Claire. She is my future. My dark cloud's silver lining. I can provide her with what she's missing in life, just as she can replace what was taken from me.

As quickly as it began, my reflection time is over, the flame extinguished. I feel so much better.

Almost time to leave. I take one last look at the house. I've spent the worst time in my life here, and yet, I'm going to miss the person I was in this place. Not enough to turn back on The Plan now, though—nothing could make me do that.

There's a glass sitting by the sink. I fill it with water from the tap, and drink. I need to get out of my head, return to the moment and what I need to do.

A sound from behind startles me, and I almost choke.

I put down the glass, waiting to see if I hear it again. Maybe it's just my mind playing tricks on me.

Sure enough, I hear it. A knock.

Someone is at my front door.

THIRTY-FOUR

EMMA

The emptiness inside is expanding, is almost as endless as the October night sky. The rain has paused, but its presence remains, muddying the soil at the side of the road, where my car is parked.

As promised, several cars start making their way down the narrow country road, their lights beaming. The solitude of the moment is lost, replaced again with chaos. The cars spread out, parking along the side of the road. One of the officers steps out of his car and approaches me.

"Do you want one of the other officers to take you back to the house?" he asks. Random flashes of red and blue are the only light to hit his face.

"No," I say, pulling down the sleeves of my jacket. "I'm waiting for Detective Sanchez."

Maybe it's because she's a woman, a mother, but I sense she's the only person I can really trust. Finally, another car makes its way down the narrow path. Sanchez steps out, comes toward me. She's holding a radio close to her lips.

"We got the driver," she says to me, hopeful. "We stopped him as he was pulling out of the fields."

"And?"

Behind her, more officers exit their vehicles, looking around the scene for any clues. Everything happened so quickly. I can't imagine they'll find anything useful. The man was here, then he was gone, and it brought me no closer to finding my daughter. My only hope is that maybe she's still inside his car. Or perhaps, he'll admit where she is.

"We searched the vehicle. It's clean."

"What's that mean?" I ask, although I fear I already know the answer.

"Claire isn't in the car." Her voice sounds defeated, but she keeps trying to remain positive. "But the man is in custody. We'll question him, see what we can figure out."

Claire wasn't in the kidnapper's car. He never had any intention of bringing her here. The one thing I wanted from him—my daughter—is still missing. But there might be something else. Maybe he has an accomplice, and he can tell the police where Claire is.

For more than an hour, this ransom drop has been the entire focus of the investigation—I refuse to believe nothing valuable can come from this.

"We need to leave the scene," Sanchez says. "I'll have another officer drive your car back to the house."

"Tell me what you know first."

"We'll discuss it back at the house," she says, walking past me.

I remain where I'm standing, refusing to be brushed off. "No, I want to know now. Who is the man you arrested? Does he have any idea where Claire is?"

Sanchez stops but doesn't turn immediately. She's avoiding telling me what she knows.

"I don't believe he knows anything about Claire."

"What do you mean? What about the ransom?"

"I could be wrong. This guy will be taken to the station and questioned thoroughly, but based on his statement when we arrested him, he never had her."

"I don't understand. What did he say?"

"He said he heard about the missing child on the news. Received the AMBER alert on his phone like everyone else in the area. He needed money, so he decided to stage a ransom, thinking this would be an easy way to get fast cash."

That emptiness inside me is changing, hardening into something else. Anger.

"He's lying. He's only saying that because he was caught."

"There will be more questioning at the station—"

"He called my house. He knew her name."

"All your information was already reported."

"There was a scream! A little girl screamed on the phone. You heard it."

"He pulled a soundbite off YouTube. He wanted to appear convincing. It's the same reason he brought the bundle of clothes. He thought it would distract you long enough for him to get away. Idiot."

"Let me see a picture," I beg. "Maybe that will trigger something. He might look like the person in the video."

"We can't make out anything about the person in the video. We've already—"

"Just let me look!" I shout.

I'm not willing to give up, to admit that the past hours have been nothing but a waste of time.

She pulls up a picture on her phone and hands it over.

When I see the face on the screen, it feels as though someone has punched me hard in the stomach. My reaction is the same, bending over, trying hard to find a breath that refuses to come. Suddenly, everything seems impossible.

"Are you sure this is the man who was here just now?"

She seems surprised. "Do you recognize him?"

"Yes. His name is Darren," I say, breathless. "He's Sarah's boyfriend."

THIRTY-FIVE

I've known Sanchez for only hours, and in that amount of time, I feel as though I've come to understand her. But I don't think I've come across this particular expression.

Shock.

"Are you sure?"

"Yes. His name is Darren Pierce. He's dating Sarah, my friend from the school."

She looks back at her phone, as though she's cross-checking names and facts, making sure she understands completely.

"Sarah, the one who was watching Claire when she was abducted, is in a relationship with this man?"

She holds out the phone again, but I don't have to look at his picture again to know. I'm absolutely certain.

"Yes. I mean, I think they're in the middle of a breakup. Or a fight. Something. But they've been together for several years. It's definitely him."

"This changes things," she mumbles, typing something into her phone. "If you know this man, does this mean Claire knows him, too?"

"Yes. I mean, they have met only a few times. I'm much

closer with Sarah than I am Darren," I say. "I never really liked him."

Now, I hate him. I don't know if I've ever felt so much rage toward another person. At best, he tried to extort money from me during my most desperate moment. At worst, he took my daughter.

"Do you still believe what he said? About the whole thing being a hoax?"

"We won't know anything until we question him. But now we know he wasn't just after money. He had a connection to your daughter. He very well could have taken her and left her with someone while he picked up the ransom."

Something inside my chest flutters, hope that maybe this wasn't a lost cause, that this ransom ordeal will bring Claire back to me, but just as quickly, that euphoric feeling hardens into despair. If Darren did take Claire, and she's not with him, who could he have left her with? If his only motive was to get money, wouldn't he have brought her with him? He could have handed her off and left with the money, but he didn't.

"We need to talk to Darren, fast. Find out where he might have left Claire."

Sanchez slides her phone into her pocket and pulls her coat tighter. "I'm heading to the station. I'll question Darren and Sarah. See what we can find out."

"I'm coming, too."

"No." She holds out a hand, her voice firm. "You did a great job tonight, but you've done your part. Now it's time for us to start asking questions, see where it leads us."

I feel so helpless I want to scream. "What am I supposed to do? I can't just sit at home waiting for answers."

"That's what you have to do. I'm sorry. I know how helpless you must feel, but we can only take this one step at a time. We'll see what they have to say, and we'll go from there."

She starts to walk away, but I call after her. "Wait, you said you're going to question Sarah, too?"

"Yes. She's already at the station, giving a statement about what really happened when she was supposed to be watching Claire."

"You don't think Sarah and Darren are in on this together?"

Sanchez has a blank look on her face, like she's waiting for me to make the connection myself, but I'm already so emotional, I'm not sure I'm thinking straight.

"This doesn't look good for your friend," she says. "She's already lied to us once in this investigation. Her negligence could be the reason Claire was taken in the first place. Now her boyfriend has been arrested for demanding a ransom."

"I know she lied," I say. "I know Darren is a deadbeat and an asshole, but Sarah... she wouldn't be involved in something like this."

Sanchez forms her mouth into a thin line, exhales through her nose. "No one wants to believe they know someone who would do something like this, but it's usually closer to home than you think. In fact, it usually takes someone we know to hurt us like this."

I remember how betrayed I felt when I realized Sarah had let Claire out of her sight and lied to me about it, but I still can't believe this was all part of some elaborate scheme she and Darren cooked up together.

Then I remember catching her on the porch, smoking again, a phone at her ear. She said she was talking to Darren. Was he using the information she gave him to trick me? Or were they working on a plan together? One of them with Claire, the other with me, watching my every move. Another brutal betrayal, one I can almost feel tightening around my heart.

"Emma, are you okay?"

Sanchez is still standing beside me, her voice calm and soothing.

"She wouldn't do this to me," I whisper, my voice convincing no one, not even myself. "She wouldn't."

"I'll have a police officer take you back to your house. You can wait there with your family. You'll be the first to know when I have something concrete."

I'm only half-listening to what she's saying, my head and heart overwhelmed.

"I can't go home again," I say. "Not without Claire."

She places her hand on my shoulder, walking me in the direction of my car.

"Go home and rest," she says. "There's nothing more you can do here."

THIRTY-SIX

The cluster of vehicles gets smaller, until I can only barely see their lights. Alone in the car with an unnamed police officer, I'm comforted by the sight of the world at night, even if there are a slew of unanswered questions left in the darkness.

On one hand, I feel so stupid, like I should have known Sarah was behind this all along. She was the person who was supposed to be watching Claire when she disappeared. She deliberately left her and lied to me about it. And now her boyfriend has been arrested for trying to demand a ransom. Any outsider looking in—Sanchez and the other investigators— would pin her as the culprit in a second.

But then I think about the person I know and not just the circumstances laid out in front of me. Sarah and I have been friends for years. She has known Claire since she was an infant. Sarah loves Claire. She works with small children every day. I can't imagine she would harm any child, let alone mine. Even if Darren is behind the ransom, my gut tells me Sarah isn't involved.

I don't know the officer driving the vehicle, can hardly tell if he's been at the house, or arrived at the cornfields with all the others, but he's the sounding board at my disposal.

"When will we hear back from Sanchez?" I ask. "I want to know what Sarah and Darren are saying."

He moves uncomfortably in his seat. Before this, we hadn't said a word to each other. I think he was happy to keep pretending I wasn't here.

"I don't know the details," he said. "Sanchez told me to take you home, and she'll send information as soon as she can."

Waiting. More and more waiting. Part of me wants to grab the wheel and race to the police station myself. Let me in front of Sarah and Darren. I'd get to the truth of what's happened, if I only had the chance.

"I know this didn't pan out how we hoped," the officer says, his voice growing braver, "but we aren't done."

"We've wasted almost two hours—"

"There are other leads we can follow. They're pulling up other security videos, following other tips that have come in online—"

"But there's nothing concrete! No one can tell me what happened to Claire."

"Nothing is concrete until it is," he says. "Someone out there knows something."

The sounds outside the car change. We're back on the highway. Away from the accident site and the failed ransom attempt. I lean my head against the window, the glass cool against my forehead. I close my eyes, think back to this morning.

I wish I could say that I cherished every moment. That I took the time to memorize Claire's smile, committed to memory everything she said. That we laughed over waffles and made a mess of the kitchen. That before we got into the car, I gave her a big hug, told my daughter how much I loved her.

But that's not what happened. Our mornings are never

ideal. Usually, it's the most stressful part of the day. Me shouting orders at Claire to get ready, as I hurriedly try to brush my own teeth and comb my hair. We rarely share a decent breakfast together. I'm usually handing over a cold pop-tart, watching the minutes tick by on my watch, afraid I'll be late.

Claire appears in my mind, rushing to the car with her backpack on her shoulders. Rush, rush, rush. Why couldn't any of us just slow down? I'd give anything to be ten minutes late this morning, if it meant I could spend a little more time with her. We'd all act differently if we knew how important these final moments were. But we don't know, so instead, we act as humans do. We take what we love for granted.

I've learned this lesson the hard way.

When I open my eyes, we're still on the highway, headed in the direction of my house. I wonder what the scene will look like when we arrive. Will cops still be scurrying around our home? Will Steven and Piper still be there? Have they already been told about the botched ransom attempt?

As we stall at the next red light, I look in the direction of the elementary school. It's nestled behind a winding drive, but I can still catch a glimpse of the building in the distance. It's after eight o'clock. At this time, the place should be deserted, and yet, even from this distance, I can see a flurry of activity, the lights from lampposts shining off the top of the cars.

"Who's at the school?" I ask.

The officer looks in that direction. "I don't know."

"It looks like there are cars. No one should be there at this hour."

"Maybe it's the cleaning staff?"

"No. They don't work on Friday nights," I say. "Pull into the parking lot."

"We should get back to the house—"

"Please," I beg.

Reluctantly, the officer steers right, driving in the direction of North Ridge Elementary.

Sure enough, the parking lot is almost full. The school building gives off an eerie quality when no one is there, all the classroom lights shut off. And yet, the lobby doors are propped open, a stale yellow glow illuminating the lobby.

"Is there some kind of event going on?" the police officer asks, for the first time interested.

I shake my head, unbuckling as soon as the car is in park. I rush toward the gray double doors.

The lobby is full. Adults are standing around, passing out papers and water bottles. Against the back wall is an unfolded card table. Laura stands behind it. She's rummaging through papers when she sees me and stops.

"Emma, my goodness. What are you doing here?"

"We saw the lights from the road," I say. I don't have the energy to tell her about everything else that has happened. "What's going on?"

Laura looks around the room. "When parents heard what happened, they wanted to help. We decided to gather here. We've had groups searching the woods between here and the pumpkin patch."

"Searching?"

"We're hoping maybe she just wandered off," she says, and I remember she doesn't know about the video proving Claire was kidnapped. She continues, "Or maybe we'll find something else. Anything that might tell us where she is."

I look around the crowded room. "I can't believe this many people showed up."

"There's even more out looking. Jack. Anna. Ben. We've all been taking turns."

"They're all out searching?"

Laura nods. "We switch around every hour. It's almost time for their group to get back. Everyone is desperate to find her,

Emma. We reached out to Sarah, but she said she was with you."

Sarah. Hearing her name hurts. Laura has no idea our friend and co-worker is presently being questioned about involvement in Claire's disappearance, that Sarah's boyfriend just tried to extort me. I still can't believe it myself. Then again, Sarah didn't mention anything to me about our group meeting at the school to help search. Maybe she didn't want to add anything else to my plate, or perhaps she wanted me to stay focused on the ransom drop. I still can't decide whether Sarah could be behind that or not.

"Sarah is at the station," I say, "answering questions about what happened at McCallister's."

"The police have questioned all of us, too," Laura says, unaware how different the situation with Sarah is. She looks down at the papers, fingering one, and handing it over. "I typed up this."

On the front of the paper is Claire's most recent school picture. Beneath that, are bullet points listing all the pertinent information about her disappearance. Where she was last seen. When she was reported missing. All the details of what she was wearing.

"Laura, I don't know what to say. Thank you for doing this."

She looks down. "I wasn't the one who brought everyone here."

"Then, who did?"

As I say this, Danica Callaway walks into the center of the lobby. She's holding a stack of the flyers in her hands.

"Okay, everyone. Before your group heads out, leave your name and where you're headed with Ms. Bailey. It's important we know where everyone is. Keep your phones on you, in case you need to call the police. And we have extra water bottles and flashlights if you need them. It's dark out there. Stay safe."

She stops talking when she catches sight of me. She hands

off the flyers to another parent and walks over, wrapping her arms around me.

"I'm so sorry this has happened," she says, "but we're doing whatever we can to bring Claire home."

Flashes of our interaction at the pumpkin patch reel through my mind. Her confusion when she learned Katy was missing, her anger that I prevented her from helping. Her gratitude when I delivered her daughter safe, back into her arms.

"You don't have to do this," I tell her. "You should be at home, with your daughter."

When she speaks, there are tears in her eyes. "You left yours so you could find mine. And instead of thanking you, I lashed out at you—"

"You were worried. And scared." I pause. "I understand what you were feeling now."

"I have my daughter back. Because of you. This is the least I can do."

"Claire isn't missing. She was kidnapped." Saying the words out loud makes the situation real, makes my stomach knot in anguish. "They have her abduction on camera. I'm not sure when it will be released."

"Oh, Emma." Danica covers her mouth with a hand. "That's not going to stop us from looking. We still might be able to find something, anything, that will help."

"I don't know what to say." My voice is breaking. "Thank you."

"I can't imagine what you're feeling, but I got a glimpse of it earlier. No mother should have to go through this." She wraps her arms around me again. "But we're in this together. You're not alone."

My first reaction is to push her away. All I've been is alone, ever since David died. It's been me and Claire against the world, waging a battle against all we've lost. But as I look around the room of concerned people, some friends and acquaintances, other co-workers and the parents of former students, I realize maybe I don't have to be. Alone, that is.

Even though this is the loneliest I've ever felt, the most desperate situation I can imagine, maybe I don't have to keep the world at a distance.

Maybe what I need to do is let others in.

THIRTY-SEVEN

When we arrive back at the house, Steven and Piper are sitting in the living room. They both stand when they see me enter.

"What happened?" Piper asks.

They must know the ransom drop was unsuccessful, even if they don't have all the details.

"Claire wasn't there," I say, defeated, barely summoning the energy for the next part. "The person who called in the ransom was a man named Darren. He's... Sarah's boyfriend."

"Sarah," Steven repeats. "As in the woman who called us?"

"Yes."

My eyes are glued to the floor, afraid to take in another person's reaction. Sanchez already made me feel foolish enough for thinking my friend wouldn't be involved.

"My goodness," Piper says, coming over and pulling me in for a well-meaning, albeit stiff, embrace. "I can't imagine she'd do that to you. I'm so sorry, Emma."

"We don't know that she was in on it."

Even though I'm not looking at either one of them, their silence tells me they have the same stance as Sanchez. The odds that Darren would be involved without Sarah are slim.

"Do you think that's why she reached out to us?" Steven says, at last. "Because she knew we'd have the funds to pay the ransom?"

It feels like something inside my chest is breaking. I hadn't thought of this, even if I probably should have. Sarah was the one who insisted I reach out to my in-laws. When I turned her down, she called them herself. Could this have been her plan? Get money and bring Claire back home? If so, why isn't Claire here?

Sanchez's words return to me: *It usually takes someone we know to hurt us like this.*

"I don't know. Sarah made many mistakes today," I say, reluctantly. "But I can't imagine she would do something like this. Darren is a different story. If he wanted money, I'm not sure there are many people he wouldn't hurt to get it."

Another tense silence fills the room. There's very little left to say. All we can do is wait, hopefully for answers, although there's the very real possibility they may never come.

Piper stands, pulling on my hands to try and get me to do the same.

"Come on, let me make you something to eat. What could I get you? A sandwich? Maybe heat up some leftovers?"

"I can't eat anything right now."

"When's the last time you ate?"

I try to recall. I think I took a couple of bites of the hot dog while we were at McCallister's, before we received word Katy was missing. I've not thought of food since then. I'm not sure I've even had much to drink.

"You're looking pale," Piper continues. "You'll want to keep your energy up, for when Claire comes home."

She's trying to stay positive, but everything feels hopeless. Eating a sandwich won't do anything to make me feel better. But Piper is right. I certainly feel like shit. My head is throbbing, and every time I stand or sit, the joints in my arms and legs ache. I probably am dehydrated, and maybe a little sustenance can carry me over a few more hours. Who knows how long I'll have to remain focused?

"Sure," I give in. "I'll take a sandwich."

Piper appears delighted that I've relented, and hurries into the kitchen. She weaves between police officers, looking in each cabinet and drawer for what she might need. It strikes me this is the first time she's ever been in our house.

"It's getting chilly," Steven says, standing. "I might start a fire."

I don't say anything. I think Piper, Steven, all of us are trying to keep ourselves busy until Sanchez returns. The officers inside the house pay us little attention, either remaining eerily quiet, or having hushed conversations among themselves. Every now and then, the rattle of a police radio grabs my attention, but no useful information comes over the airwaves.

"Here," Piper says, coming up behind me. She's holding a peanut butter sandwich on a plate. "Maybe this will make you feel better."

"Thanks," I say, my eyes wandering to the fire across the way. Steven is standing in front of it, his back to me. He's so still, you'd think he's some type of statue. I wonder what he's thinking right now. If, like me, he wishes David were here with us. As always, it seems everything would be easier to understand, all problems easier to solve, if he were still around.

I've finished my last bite of the sandwich—turns out, my body was hungrier than my emotions led me to believe—when a familiar voice trails in from outside. Detective Sanchez is back. I can hear her speaking on the front porch with another officer.

I stand so quickly, my plate falls out of my lap, and glides to the floor.

Sanchez meets me at the front door, just as I was about to follow her outside.

"You weren't gone long," I say. "What did Darren say? Did he tell you anything about Claire?"

"Maybe we should take a seat."

But now that there's a little food in my body, I'm antsy. The last thing I want to do is sit. I have so much energy, I'm bouncing from one foot to the other. I barely move over enough to let Sanchez all the way inside the room.

"I need to know what Darren said," I tell her. "And Sarah."

Sanchez sighs. "He's been questioned extensively. I talked to him myself, for almost an hour. But despite your personal connection, my theory back at the ransom site still stands. I don't believe Darren is involved."

"Of course, he's involved!" I correct her. "He's the one who made the ransom call."

"A crime has been committed. There's no getting around that." She pauses. "But he doesn't have Claire, and I don't believe he knows who does. He was only after money. Said something about needing to pay back his brother in order to get his job back."

"What's wrong with people?" Piper says, outraged. "Who could even think about money at a time like this?"

That's easy for her to say. People like Steven and Piper never have to think about money. It's the answer to all their problems. They can't even imagine a problem like this, where no amount of money in the world can remedy it. I ignore them, focusing again on Sanchez.

"How can you be so sure? He knows me. He could have been planning this all along as a way to get money."

"If that's the case, we would know where Claire is right now. He has no reason to make things worse for himself."

"Maybe there's another reason he's staying quiet." There's a sinking feeling in my stomach. "Maybe something went wrong. Claire could be hurt."

"We've explored all the options, but I genuinely think this is an asshole who saw an opportunity and jumped on it. The fact he knows you only made him think he'd have a better chance of getting away with it."

"What about Sarah?"

Sanchez's face hardens. "I spoke with her. When I told her Darren made the ransom call, she was genuinely upset. She became physically ill. Suspects can be skilled liars, but you usually can't fake a reaction like that. I think you were right about your friend. She wasn't involved."

What should be a small victory is overshadowed by the many questions hammering through my brain. There's no way we can be back at square one, no closer to finding Claire.

"He's not involved," I say in disbelief. My voice sounds desperate when I address Sanchez again. "He doesn't know anything?"

"This guy was trying to profit off your tragedy, and for that he'll get slapped with interfering with an investigation and anything else we can charge him with." She pauses. "But I don't believe he's the person who took Claire."

"Then where is she?" My breaths are coming harder and faster now. "We've been focusing on this ransom for hours. He's the only person who has contacted us. If he didn't kidnap Claire, then who did?"

Maybe my eyes have adjusted to the darkness. Or maybe I'm standing too close to Detective Sanchez. Whatever it is, I now have a full view of her face. The expression on it. She pities me.

"We don't know."

It hits me then. I don't know where my daughter is. Sanchez doesn't know. No one does. She could be anywhere, and there's a very real possibility that whoever took her has no intention of reaching out. Ever. I could never know what happened to my daughter. This realization is so harrowing, my knees buckle. I fall forward, landing hard on the wooden floors.

THIRTY-EIGHT

After standing and finding my balance, I exit the room, but instead of going upstairs to my own bedroom, which is just across the hall from Claire's, I go to the music room. It's like I'm being pulled there, in a trance. My hands glide over the smooth surface of David's guitar. I pick at one of the strings, until it vibrates beneath my fingers.

How would David react? I can guess, based on the way he behaved in the grocery store that day, he'd be calmer than I am. Then again, Claire has been missing for much longer than she was then, and I have no idea who has her.

Of course, this never would have happened if David were here. He never would have let Claire out of his sight. He would have made sure when he was doing his own work that he wasn't distracted. He would have been on the field trip today, so that I could have done my job while he gave Claire all the attention she deserves.

I need him here. I've always needed him here. And I took his presence for granted when he was alive, just like I took advantage of my time with Claire this morning, rushing her out the door. Arguing with her about that silly ribbon in her hair.

"Did David ever tell you about the time we got in trouble for shoplifting?"

I turn quickly to see Steven standing in the doorway, the same spot where Piper had stood before I left for the ransom drop. There must be something about this room. It draws all of us in.

"We were at the old music store downtown," he continues, his gaze taking in each guitar carefully. He is smiling. "Our mom took us in there to get my first guitar. I was six, and David was only four. I don't remember much about the trip, until we got stopped walking out the door.

"Turns out David had pocketed a handful of guitar picks. You know, the little cheap ones they keep in a jar by the checkout counter? I was all excited about my new carrying case, and Mom was busy paying the cashier. Neither of us noticed."

"And he got in trouble for that?"

"The cashier tried. It was some teenage kid. A real Karen in the making. Probably the closest to a scandal she ever experienced the whole time she worked there. David cried the whole way home because he didn't understand why he couldn't have them all."

"No," I say, looking back at the shag carpet. "He never told me."

"We used to laugh about it with my parents. How David couldn't wait to grow up. He never wanted to be a kid. He always wanted to join what I was doing. Help Dad around the house or Mom in the kitchen. He couldn't wait to start life."

That lump in my throat returns. Just when I think I can't be anymore heartbroken over Claire, I'm reminded that David is gone too, and my grief compounds.

"He couldn't wait to settle down, either," Steven continues. "I mean, don't get me wrong. We had fun when we were younger, but the moment he met you, he couldn't wait to trade in his bachelor card. I couldn't understand it at first. How a person could be so sure. Especially someone younger than me. But David always knew what he wanted, and he knew he wanted you."

Part of my heart wants to burst with happiness, but those same sensations turn sour at the thought I'll never again get to hold my husband in my arms.

"Why are we talking about David?"

"Because I miss him. I never get to talk about him anymore. I mean, Piper is always willing to listen, but she never got the chance to meet him. Thankfully, she never met the person I was before he died. It feels like I'm different now, somehow."

"I don't like talking about him."

"I can tell."

The words aren't harsh, but they hit me like a palm across the face. I look at him, crossing my arms over my chest. "What does that mean?"

"Come on, Emma. It's obvious you've been avoiding us—avoiding me—ever since David died."

"I've been trying to survive." I look away. "You can tell how that's worked out."

"I know you blame me for what happened."

His voice is low, serious. The words strike me like I've been hit with a stone. I've long believed Steven thinks this, and for two years I've let him continue to. It's easier than admitting the truth about what happened that night.

"I never should have let him leave," he continues. "If I'd only bit my tongue—"

"Stop." I turn abruptly, taking in all the pain and suffering on Steven's face. I look away. "I don't want to talk about that night."

But already, my mind is going back there. I'm sitting with a young Claire in the massive basement at Steven's house. She's crawling around on the rug. I'm watching her every move, so that she won't run into a piece of furniture and break something. I'm singing to her, trying to drown out the sounds of the brothers' voices from up above. They're in an argument. Again.

Now I'm picturing the look on David's face when he emerges from the staircase. Seeing the hurt on his face. I watch as David grabs the car keys, storms off.

I close my eyes and shake my head, trying to dislodge the memory from my brain.

"What happened to David isn't your fault," I tell Steven, in the present.

He isn't listening, his eyes locked in on another instrument. Maybe, like me, he's forcing himself not to think about that night. "As awful as this situation is, I'm happy to be back here. I'm happy to be around his things again."

"Well, I hate being around them," I say, turning to face him. "I don't need reminders that he's gone. I feel it every morning, every night. Every time something goes wrong. Every time something goes right. That awful feeling is always there, but he never is."

"He wouldn't have wanted this, you know. You closing yourself away from the rest of the world."

"That's not what I've been doing!"

I'm offended by the suggestion. Steven and Piper have no concept of what the real world is like. Their privilege and wealth have shielded them from it. If something tragic were to befall them, they could lock themselves away in hiding to deal with their grief. Or they could escape it. Book a trip somewhere and *Eat, Pray, Love* their way through the pain.

The real world isn't like that. My life isn't like that. My husband died, and I still had to go to work two weeks later. I had to scramble to pay our mortgage at the beginning of the next month. Overnight, I was handed the responsibilities of two people, and forced to juggle them alone, all the while maintaining a smile so Claire couldn't see the pain I was truly feeling. I didn't have time to care about Steven's feelings or anyone else's—I was already fully occupied with looking after myself and my daughter.

"You don't know what we've been through. You can't even imagine."

"I can't." He pauses. "I can't imagine what you're going through now, but I'm here. And I'm trying to help."

"Talking about David won't do anything to help us find Claire."

"Maybe it won't, but I've waited long enough." He pauses. "I know it feels like you're the only one who lost someone that day, but you're not. I lost my brother. My best friend. And even though I didn't know it at the time, I lost any future connection I had with the family he would have done anything to protect."

Tears build in my eyes. I'm filled with anger, sadness, and for the first time, shame. He's right. David's loss tore my life apart, but it wasn't the only life destroyed.

"It hurts seeing you. It hurts talking about him. Any part of David hurts me now."

"Claire is part of David," he says. "And I know you love her."

I lower my head, try to swallow down another cry. "You must think I'm an awful mother."

"Why would you say that?"

"It's what people on *The Meghan Lachlan Show* are saying."

"The media doesn't know anything about you."

"But you said it yourself. I've tried to keep Claire away from any memories of her father. I tried to protect her, but I couldn't even keep her safe."

"We're going to find Claire, and when we do, maybe we'll finally have a chance to make things right."

"How can you be so hopeful?"

"Because the only other option is to give up," he says. "And I'm not going to do that."

Steven is right. I've put so much distance between us since David's death that I forgot how close their bond with each other once was. In fact, I refused to be the one to tell him David died. I asked one of the police officers to make the notification. I couldn't bear to see the look on his face, the blame I already felt burning hotter.

"Tonight, when we went on the ransom run, we drove by the place where the accident happened. I've not been back there since he died."

"I haven't either." He looks away. "But I think about him every day. And I can't help feeling he'd be mad at the both of us for letting our family fall apart the way it has."

"Excuse me, Emma?" It's Sanchez. "I think we might have found something."

And suddenly, amid the ongoing loss, I feel a spark of what Steven was talking about.

I feel hope.

THIRTY-NINE

We're gathered around the dining room table again. An officer is typing into a laptop, pulling up an image.

"It could be nothing," Sanchez warns us, "but we want you to look at something. See if anything stands out to you."

The officer pulls up a slideshow of pictures. He pauses on each one before clicking on the next. There are eight in total.

"What am I supposed to be looking at?"

"Just try to focus," Sanchez says. "And tell me if anything looks familiar."

Nothing looks familiar. I'm not even sure where the pictures were taken. It's on some highway, but the angle of the camera is awkward. I can only make out part of the vehicles as they pass, as if photos are taken in sporadic intervals.

Then something catches my eye. In the third photo, there's a light-colored sedan. In the back seat, there appears to be someone. The image is blurry, but I can tell that it's a ponytail.

"It looks like there is a girl in the back seat."

Sanchez smiles. "That's what we think, too."

"But it could be anyone," Piper says. "How can you tell it's Claire?"

"This photo was taken on the highway leading away from the pumpkin patch. A red-light cam picked it up. We've been cross-checking cars on this highway with the ones that were caught on camera in McCallister's parking lot. This is the only match we've got so far."

"So, this could be Claire?"

"It's a lead we can follow," she says. "And take a look at the next picture."

The officer clicks over to the next photo and zooms in. At the bottom of the screen, is a license plate.

"You can identify the car?"

"We can try," Sanchez says. "It gives us something, at least."

"What do we do now?"

"I know you're frustrated with hearing me say this, but we wait. We'll look into this. It's the most promising lead we've had yet. If we're lucky, we'll be able to identify the owner of the vehicle. At the very least, we can look for this car on other local cameras. It might give us an idea of where they're headed."

"And if it's not Claire?" Steven says.

"We'll stay hopeful," Sanchez says.

This could be another false lead. It could be nothing at all.

But right now, it's something—anything—bringing me one step closer to my daughter.

"I told you," Steven says, squeezing my shoulder. "We can't lose hope."

And as much as I hate to admit it, I know he's right.

As I stare again at the blurry image on the screen, a weak smile spreads across my face.

FORTY

"There's good news and bad news," Sanchez says.

Another thirty minutes has passed since she showed me the video of the car on the highway. My insides start reeling again. A steep high followed by a deep low.

"What is it?"

"We ran the plates, but it belongs to a rental."

"Which means—"

"We can't identify the driver just yet," she says, a tinge of defeat in her voice. "We're sending officers to the rental place right now. It came from the airport, which means it's a twenty-four-hour service. We should know something soon. Hopefully get the guy on camera so we can see his face."

"That sounds like all good news to me," Steven says.

"It is, really. We're moving forward, which is what counts. I just wish I had more answers to give," Sanchez says. "But the fact that the kidnapper rented a car before going to the pumpkin patch gives us a little more insight. It makes me think this wasn't a random abduction. They went to McCallister's intending to snatch a child. It appears there's more planning involved with this than we might have originally thought. We have to consider the possibility that Claire has been this guy's target all along."

Why would someone intentionally take Claire? I thought we were working under the theory that someone took advantage of Katy's disappearance to snatch a random child. Even if the kidnapper did rent a car, that still could be possible. But the fact there was a certain level of planning involved at least opens a door to the idea that Claire was his target.

Another thought strikes me, and I sit up.

"When I found Katy in the cornfields, she had something with her. A soda can."

"Why is that important?" Sanchez asks.

"I'm around kindergartners all day. Katy couldn't have opened her own soda can. Someone would have to open it for her."

"What about Laura?"

"She wouldn't have bought the children snacks before lunch. And even if she did, she's old school. Waters and crackers only. Not any of the syrupy, artificial stuff."

"So, you're saying if the girl had a soda, an adult would have given it to her?"

"Maybe Katy didn't get lost in the cornfields. Maybe someone led her there. He wasn't using the opportunity to snatch Claire. He created it!"

"I'll get one of the officers to run by Katy's house and talk to her again. Maybe there's something else she remembers but is afraid to say." Sanchez sits in front of me, resting her elbows on her lap. "In the meantime, I want you to think hard about anyone who would want to target you or your daughter, specifically."

My mind races, dozens of faces flashing through my thoughts. I interacted with countless people on today's field trip. Some of them were strangers, but others were students' parents and colleagues. I can't imagine anyone in my life would want to hurt me like this, but why would a stranger go to such lengths to kidnap *my* daughter? It must be someone I know.

I'm silent, still thinking, when Sanchez speaks again.

"Do you work with a man named Ben Shaver?"

"Of course. He's another kindergarten teacher at the school."

"Are the two of you close?"

"His classroom is right across from mine. Why are you asking?"

My entire teaching team appears in my mind. I remember the way they supported me on the anniversary of David's death. Ben was right there with them.

She sighs. "A concerned citizen mentioned his name on the tipline. They said he had a history of lashing out at the school."

The substitute. Ben's reputation was bruised by that incident, but we all rallied around him, like we always do.

"That was a misunderstanding. A former substitute made a complaint against him, but Ben didn't do anything wrong."

"Would you say this man has a temper?"

If I'm being truthful, yes, he does. But Ben wouldn't have any reason to hurt Claire. The few times I've seen his temper, it's because he was defending one of our students.

"What happened then doesn't have anything to do with Claire's disappearance. It was a one-time incident."

"So, you aren't aware of his issue at a previous school?"

"What are you talking about?"

"Before he came to North Ridge, he was let go from his previous position for getting into an altercation with an administrator."

"A physical altercation?" Steven asks, suddenly interested.

"I don't know all the details," Sanchez admits, "but it's an interesting history. Especially since he was on the field trip today and around Claire."

"He was helping me," I point out. "He wouldn't have had the opportunity to take Claire."

I reconsider his demeanor when we were searching for Katy. Ben was hesitant about getting the police involved, even after it was clear she wasn't in the barn. When we were in the cornfields, he was the one who said we should split up. Did he *want* me to be the one to find her so it wouldn't put more suspicion on him? Could he have known Katy's disappearance was only a ruse, something to distract me? All these questions are rising from my paranoia, and I can't believe I'm aiming them at a man I thought I could trust.

"Did you see him on the premises after you became aware Claire was missing?"

"No," I realize. "He'd already headed back to school with the others."

"Then he might know more than he's telling us."

"Laura said he was at the school, helping with the search."

"Did you see him?"

"No." I stand, begin pacing the room. If Claire was taken by someone I know, it forces me to reconsider every interaction I've had with those around me. The slightest offense or disagreement. "I don't like doing this. Sarah, now Ben. It's driving me crazy. I don't know who to trust."

"I know this is difficult. I'm only trying to investigate every possibility. His name was mentioned, and it was a theory I wanted to run by you." She turns to Steven and Piper. "Let's think about the rest of the family. Has anything strange happened to you in recent weeks?"

"They have nothing to do with this," I say. "I mean, if someone was wanting to hurt them, they wouldn't go after Claire to do it."

"It's not a likely scenario, but you never know. We need to explore all avenues." She turns back to the couple, her eyes narrowing. "Can you think of anyone that might have a problem with either one of you?"

Steven clears his throat. "Sure, I've had a few disagreements with people concerning my business. But Emma's right. None of those people would target Claire."

"A few disagreements about your business." Sanchez sounds interested. "Tell me more about that."

Steven shifts in his seat. Piper scoots closer to him. "I've done well for myself in the past couple of years. Made some good investments. People always say it takes money to make money, and now that I have a little bit, I've been setting up my own company."

Sanchez is growing impatient. "Doing what?"

"It's tech stuff. A little hard to explain—"

"My husband is the IT guy for the chamber of commerce," she says, sitting back. "Try me."

"It's domain names," Piper speaks up. "He's been purchasing domain names in bulk and selling them to the highest bidder."

"See? That doesn't sound too hard to figure out. So, what's the trouble with that?" Sanchez asks.

"Customers can get upset when they realize we're the stopping point between them and their next great idea," Steven says. "It's made us some enemies."

"I didn't know you guys even had a business," I say, looking back and forth between my in-laws.

"How bad are these enemies?" Sanchez asks, redirecting the conversation.

"I think we need to tell them," Piper whispers, "about last weekend."

Sanchez sits up straighter now. "What happened last weekend?"

Steven gives Piper a look. He's clearly irritated she brought it up. "We had a break-in at our house."

"Was this reported?"

"Yes," Piper says. "Thankfully, our alarm system went off, so they couldn't take much. Most of what was stolen was in the office."

"I'm guessing that's where you keep the documents concerning your business."

"Yes," he says. "Which is why I believed it was related to that."

"But it's also where we keep personal records," Piper adds. "Social security cards. Tax records. Family documents."

"You're saying, if someone was looking for anything concerning Claire—"

"They'd go into that room," Piper finishes Sanchez's sentence for her. "I know it's a stretch, but it could be something, right?"

"No!" Steven insists. "Claire doesn't have any connection to our business."

"But we do have her information." She looks at me now. "Claire is our sole beneficiary if anything were to happen to us. Maybe someone saw that in our records."

"What are you getting at, Piper?" Steven is nearly shouting. "You can't really think this has anything to do with Claire's disappearance."

"I don't know, but the detective says we need to consider all angles—"

"Let her look into things. Not you."

In the few times I've been around Steven and Piper together, I've never seen them argue. Tensions are high for all of us, but it's obvious how offended he is that Piper brought any of this up. Could he have something to hide? I recall the uneasy feeling I had when they first arrived tonight. They've done nothing but offer support since they've been here, but maybe there's more they haven't told me.

"As the detective, I think we could look into this further."

Sanchez stands, resting her hands on her hips. "Maybe we can take a walk into the other room. You can tell me more about this break-in."

I watch as Sanchez escorts Steven outside, and my heart sinks.

The same person who gave me reason to hope is now taking it away.

FORTY-ONE

I walk outside to the back porch. Piper is standing there, staring at something in the distance. She turns when she hears my footsteps creak across the planks.

"You scared me," she says, quickly turning again. "It's pretty here at night, seeing all the lights in the distance."

"Yeah, I know."

"Maybe Steven is right. I'm spouting off when I really need to shut my mouth."

"You did the right thing. If you think someone might be using Claire to hurt Steven, it's worth investigating," I say. "I've had to reconsider stuff, too. Like what the detective was saying about Ben."

"I'm so desperate for answers. I can't imagine what you're going through."

"No. You can't."

She looks at me now, with hurt in her eyes. She looks like she's about to speak, then stops.

"What is it?" I ask.

"Nothing."

"If you have something to say—"

"Now isn't the time."

"If it's about Claire, you don't need to hold anything back."

She looks at me again, with that same sad expression. "What I was going to say isn't about Claire. It's about you."

I wait, hoping she'll find the courage to share what's on her mind.

"I know what you think of me. I know what everyone thinks of me, really. Young, blonde and dumb. Married some rich guy so I can travel around the world and carry a Birkin and try out trendy manicures. That's all you think I am."

"I didn't say that—"

"But you do. You say it all the time, when you're making your snide remarks about our lifestyle. Reminding me that I'm not a mother, like you did earlier."

A blister of shame pulsates inside me. "I'm upset right now. I didn't mean to insult you."

"I know you're hurting. That's why I didn't want to bring it up. There's so much more to worry about right now aside from our relationship," she says. "But you don't know me, Emma. And it gets tiring when the whole world thinks they have you pegged just because of the size of your husband's bank account.

"You know, people think the only reason Steven and I don't have kids is because I'm so vain. That I don't want to put up with the weight gain and the stretch marks and the lack of sleep. You want to know the real reason?"

She doesn't give me a chance to answer before continuing.

"It's because I couldn't stand the thought of something bad ever happening to them. I've lost loved ones before and it's just... the worst feeling. I've seen what Steven has gone through since David died. I see what you're going through right now. I can't imagine how my entire world would fall apart if someone took my child away from me.

"Truthfully, I think about having a baby. I used to want lots of them, actually. How much fun it would be to show them the world, to spoil them on holidays, to give Claire cousins to play with. But then I think about all the bad things that could happen, and I realize it's not worth it. I can't risk losing them, because I'm not strong like you. I'm too weak.'"

There's a lump in my throat, the shame rising. The image Piper has painted is exactly as I see her. Vain and vapid. I never considered she wants a family, that she might envy the little life Claire and I share.

"You're wrong," I tell her. "It is worth it. Even now, the pain I'm in. The fear and not knowing. I'd do it all over again, just to have the happy moments I've had with Claire."

I stop talking as a new image enters my mind. The possibility that I might never see my daughter again. That our time together might have run out, that all I'll ever have of her is the time we've already spent.

I smile.

"Claire is the best thing I've ever done in my life. The thought of losing her is unimaginable, but the joy of having her? It makes every bit of pain worth it."

Piper sniffles. "That's beautiful."

"I only wish I hadn't taken our time together for granted."

"I believe we'll get answers. There's a good team here. And it's why I spoke up about the break-in. Any theory, no matter how far-fetched, is worth exploring if it brings Claire back."

"I'm sorry for treating you and Steven like shit over the past two years. I've been so tied up in my own grief, I haven't thought about either of you. Then this happens, and you both drop everything to be here for me."

"It's what family does."

I'm reminded of my conversation with Steven in the music room, how he begged me to have hope. Piper has the same philosophy, and I'm understanding, for the first time, why the two of them are so well-suited. It isn't because they're wealthy and beautiful. It's a connection much deeper than that.

"I already apologized to Steven," I say. "I never considered his loss."

"It hasn't been easy for him, but he's finally in a place where he can remember the good times without thinking of how everything played out. We have our own ways of remembering David."

"I know. I saw what you did, at the crash site."

"The crash site?"

"I passed it tonight, when I was doing the ransom drop. It's the first time I've seen it since... well, it happened."

"Oh." She looks down, uncertain. "Yeah, Steven can't bear to go there either."

"It must have been you that put up the crosses."

"What do you mean?"

"By the road. There were memorial crosses and flowers."

"It wasn't me," she says. "I've never been there."

I replay my conversation with Steven and realize it couldn't have been him. When I told him I passed the crash site, he admitted he couldn't go there either.

If none of us have visited the scene since David died, then who has?

"You could do one thing to help me," I say to Piper. She turns to look at me, eager. "Let's go on a drive."

FORTY-TWO

Sanchez is still busy with Steven, going over any possible connection their home burglary could have to Claire's abduction. I told one of the uniformed officers at the house I needed to get some fresh air, and he didn't say much as Piper and I climbed into the front of her black Suburban. Even though I'm dependent on the police for information, I'm not being detained. I'm free to come and go as I please.

"Are you sure leaving the house is the best idea?" Piper asks, fastening her seat belt.

"We won't be gone long. It's just up the road."

"But where are we going?"

I wait until my house is distant in the rearview before I tell her. "The crash site."

Is it just me, or does her body tense? The expression on her face has changed, like she's suddenly unsure she should be taking direction from me.

"Why would we go there?"

"You said earlier you'd never been there."

"I have no desire to go," she says, flatly.

"But Steven said the same thing. That he's never been."

"What does any of this have to do with Claire?"

"During the ransom drop, I saw a memorial by the side of the road. None of us put it there."

I think back to the scene tonight. It's hard because I was trying to block out the images, and now they're all I want to see.

"What do you think any of this has to do with Claire?"

"It may have nothing to do with her," I say. "But if none of us created the memorial, I don't know who did."

Knowing Claire was specifically targeted changes everything. I'm being forced to reconsider the details of my life, the people and events in it. Whoever took Claire must know about our lives, too. David's accident may not have a direct link to Claire's abduction, but his death was the biggest challenge I've ever faced, until tonight. When I saw the memorial crosses earlier, it twisted the knife that seems permanently wedged inside my heart. Now, I'm wondering if there is something more significant about the scene, something I overlooked before.

"Maybe it's for another person all together. It's a dangerous road. David can't be the first person who lost his life there."

And yet I'm convinced that this memorial is connected to David. I try to picture the scene again.

Soon I no longer have to imagine it; we're fast approaching. Piper drives extra slow along the backroads. She's probably never been this far away from the city, and she appears nervous. Just like earlier, we're completely surrounded by black night, the headlight beams casting an eerie light on everything in front of us.

"Right here. Stop."

The car halts. Ahead, I can see the makeshift memorial on the side of the road, just to the right. I unbuckle and open the passenger side door.

"Are you sure about this?" Piper says.

There's something in her voice. Apprehension, fear. Maybe she thinks I'm starting to lose my sanity.

"I'll only be a minute. I need to see something."

I move ahead, my footsteps hitting the dull, uneven ground with a thud. I stay clear of the headlights, making sure not to cast a shadow on what I've come here to see.

Just as I remembered, there are two crosses. Ribbons tied tight around each one. The color pattern is unique. With both ribbons, the top side of the fabric is blue, while the underside is pink. In some ways, it seems too happy for something marking a person's death. Strange.

I take in the condition of the memorial. I wondered if perhaps Steven was wrong. If he, or another distant family member, put up the memorial in the days following David's death. Perhaps time and grief had made him forget. But this memorial looks new. Fresh. The wood isn't weathered or aged. Even though a storm came through earlier tonight, the ribbons are pocked with raindrops, but they're intact, not tattered and torn. This hasn't been here long, or if it has, it's been well looked after.

I take out my phone and snap a picture of the memorial before returning to the car.

Piper sits patiently behind the wheel, but she's clearly growing frustrated. "I don't understand why you needed to come here."

"Look," I say, holding out my phone. She takes a glimpse at the memorial for only a second before looking away, as though she's seen something she wishes she hadn't.

"There are two crosses."

"Two people died in the crash," I say, "but the other person wasn't local."

Piper opens her mouth, like she's about to say something, then stops. It appears our conversation with one another is going in circles.

"Don't you think there is something strange about the ribbon? The colors?"

"Different colors have different meanings. Pink for breast cancer. Purple for Alzheimer's awareness."

"What color represents a death or an accident?"

"I'm not sure. Black, I guess. Look it up."

"Definitely not pink and blue. But it has to have some meaning if someone put it there, right?"

I keep searching until I find a memorial ribbon listicle that gives the meaning behind various colors. When I get to blue and pink, I understand why the unique ribbons jogged my memory. I've seen them before, on the flower arrangement I sent Laura in the wake of her daughter's miscarriage. Pink and blue wound together.

My jaw drops. I hold out the phone for Piper to see.

"What is it?"

"This ribbon represents the loss of a child."

FORTY-THREE

I blink several times, but Dr. Meade is still here, standing on my front porch.

She smiles. "Aren't you going to invite me in?"

"Of course."

I stand back, allowing her to walk inside. It's been over a year since we had a home visit. Once she thought I was improving, she stopped coming. Why is she here now?

"Hell of a storm," I say, closing the front door. "What brings you out in this?"

"I was in the neighborhood," she says, taking a seat at the dining room table. She doesn't ask to sit. She just does. "I know that sounds crazy, at this time of night, but it's true."

"I didn't think you lived here anymore. I figured since your office moved—"

"No, I don't live here. I was in the area for work."

"Oh yeah? Another patient?"

"You know I'm not at liberty to say."

"Right, right. Just making small talk." I rush into the kitchen, making it a point to hide my face. "Can I get you something to drink?"

"A water would be nice."

Her tone is friendly. She doesn't sound suspicious. That's good. Maybe it really is just a visit. What reason could she have to suspect me? I think of the girl in the basement. The drug shouldn't wear off just yet. She'll stay quiet, I tell myself.

I come back into the room and begin a conversation. "How are you?"

"Very good. Busy with the new practice." She pauses. "I've been thinking maybe I made the wrong decision, moving so soon."

"Are you coming to me for advice now?"

"Thank you," she says, as she takes the water bottle. There's a small laugh. "No, not seeking advice. I guess, I wanted to hear your thoughts. After all, I made some of my greatest progress with you. I want to make sure I haven't made a mistake, leaving you the way I did."

"No need to worry about me." I take a sip of my own water. "You know I'd reach out if things were getting bad again."

"Are you going somewhere?"

She looks at the bags beside the door. Camping gear. I wander closer to the mess and pull out a flashlight.

"No, I was just trying to dig out this. It's an old house with faulty wiring." I smile. "Thought it might come in handy if the storm gets worse."

She doesn't say anything, but her eyes stay on me. "I talked to Doctor Ramirez. He says you've not been returning his calls."

"I've been busy with work. You know what it's like this time of the year—"

"He says you've missed your weekly appointments."

I open my mouth to speak, but quickly close it. It's better to smile first. "I've missed two appointments. And I had good reasons."

"But you've refused to schedule another one."

"That's not true. I've just been busy." I wait. "Is that why you're in the area? Did Doctor Ramirez send you to check up on me?"

"Doctor Ramirez didn't send me to do anything. I wanted to see you. We made such progress together. I don't understand why you can't do the same with Ramirez."

"Because Ramirez is a hack!" My voice comes out angry. I clear my throat, start over. "He doesn't listen to me the way you do. He knows what happened, but he doesn't really get it, you know? He's only listening to me because it's his job."

"Ramirez cares deeply for his patients. I wouldn't have left you under his supervision otherwise."

"He doesn't! It's insulting to sit in front of some guy I hardly know and share my darkest thoughts. I know good and well he won't understand."

"You barely knew me when we started working together," she reminds me.

"You earned my trust. You pulled me out of that dark place I was in. And now I'm better. I've figured out what I need to do to move on."

"Part of moving on is ongoing therapy—"

"Not with that hack it's not." I pause. "Trust me, if I can't talk about what happened with you, I'm better dealing with it on my own."

"If you don't like working with Doctor Ramirez, I can recommend other counselors in the area."

"I don't need another counselor, okay? Why aren't you listening to me?"

"What you're living with... there's no getting better. You know that. Even though you've made great gains, you need someone in your life that can help you if you backslide."

My teeth are gritted. "I'm not backsliding."

"I didn't come here to upset you. It's probably best that I leave." She stands. "Do you mind if I use your bathroom?"

"You going to check the cabinets to make sure I'm taking my meds?"

"Are you taking your meds?"

"Yes."

"Then, no. I'm not trying to deceive you."

She stands and walks down the narrow hallway leading to the bathroom. The door closes.

There's a sound. I think, maybe, footsteps. Is it the girl? Is she climbing the steps? What if she cries out? Dr. Meade must leave before The Plan is ruined. The bathroom door opens, and Meade exits.

"It's been good seeing you," she says, holding her purse in front of her. "I'll be sending over a list of other therapists in the area."

"Maybe I just haven't found the right fit."

She's almost to the front door when she stops. "I did want to ask you, have you heard anything about the little girl that went missing?"

"Girl?"

"It's been all over the news. Surely, you've seen it."

"I've been home all night."

She looks at the coatrack by the door. My jacket is wet from the rain. Muddy boot prints dirty the floors. She looks back at me.

"She attends North Ridge Elementary."

Dr. Meade doesn't know when to stop. She just keeps... thinking. And talking. When she leaves here, she won't let this go. She'll eventually put together who the girl is, and then...

"Hey, Doc?" I say, cool as a cucumber.

When she turns, I lunge at her, hitting her over the head with the flashlight. Dr. Meade stumbles, her hand going to her head. She pulls it away. Sees the blood.

I hit her again and again.

"I'm sorry," I gasp, in between licks. "But I'm not going to let you ruin this for me."

She no longer resists.
"No one is going to ruin The Plan," I say.

FORTY-FOUR

EMMA

When I rush into the kitchen, Sanchez is deep in conversation with two other officers. When she sees me, she raises her head.

"Where have you been?"

I bypass her questions, my hands shaking as I grip the phone tighter. "I think I might have something," I say.

She steps forward, giving me her full attention. "Has someone contacted you?"

"No, but I remembered something from earlier tonight."

"At the pumpkin patch?"

"No. It was something I saw during the ransom drop."

"We've already established that threat isn't connected—"

"It's not about the ransom drop. It's about something we passed on the way there. The crosses on the side of the road."

Sanchez's face relaxes. "Emma, I'm not following."

"Earlier tonight, on the way to the drop, I passed a memorial on the side of the road. It was where David had his car crash two years ago."

"David." She blinks, trying to follow. "Your husband?"

"Yes. The memorial caught my attention because I didn't put it there. And neither did Piper and Steven."

"What does any of this have to do with Claire?"

"There were ribbons tied to the crosses. Pink and blue ribbons. I looked it up and those colors symbolize the loss of a child."

It's hard to decipher what Sanchez is thinking.

"Was a child killed in your husband's accident?"

"No. There were two fatalities, but no children." I pause, my mind revisiting the scene from earlier, desperately trying to sift through the clues. "I was emotional when we drove past the scene earlier, which is why I didn't think about it. But don't you think it's strange there is a ribbon for a lost child placed at the exact same location where Claire's father died?"

"It could be." Sanchez bites her lower lip. "But it's such a small detail. One of the other family members could have simply placed a memorial."

"It's worth looking into, right? I mean, until we figure out who hired the rental car, we don't have much else."

I feel myself getting frustrated. Sanchez is right; it's such a small detail, but it's the only one I can focus on now. For whatever reason, that image of the pink and blue ribbon tied tightly around the weathered crosses refuses to leave my mind.

It seems beyond coincidence that on the same night my child was taken, I find ribbons at my husband's memorial, ribbons that, of all things, represent a lost child. No child was injured the night David died, but Claire is missing. And the person responsible targeted Claire.

"We'll look into it, okay?" Sanchez says. She puts her hand on my shoulder, turning me in the direction of the living room. "I can have one of my officers pull up the accident report. When did it happen?"

I tell her the date of the accident, spew out details I've tried to suppress for more than two years. It's surprising how easy it is to pull on the most painful event from my life now that I believe it might somehow be linked to Claire's disappearance.

When we re-enter the living room, Steven and Piper are sitting in front of the fireplace. They look up at me, a dozen different questions in their expressions.

"Rest here for a while and I'll let you know when we have more information."

Sanchez directs me to sit on the sofa, and only then do I sense the skepticism in her voice. She doesn't believe this is truly connected to Claire's disappearance. It's only the pointless ramblings of a woman desperate to find answers. Perhaps I'm starting to lose it.

As soon as she leaves the room, Steven stands, walking across the room to be closer to me.

"I'm sorry for not saying anything about the break-in earlier," he says. "I honestly don't believe it has anything to do with what happened to Claire, but I still answered all the officers' questions. If there is a connection in any way, I want to do everything in my power to help."

"What did the detective say?" Piper asks, her voice guilt-ridden. "Do they think there is a connection?"

"She didn't say anything about the burglary. I had an idea I was running past her."

"What is it?" Steven asks.

I tell him about the memorial, about the ribbon tied around the crosses.

"I know it's a long shot," I say, "but I can't ignore the fact that someone used a ribbon for a missing child at the accident scene, and now Claire is missing."

"What did Sanchez say when you told her?" Piper asks.

I sigh. "She didn't seem overly enthusiastic. I get the impression the cops think I'm starting to lose it."

"It's something small," Steven says. "But it could have a bigger meaning."

"That's what I'm hoping."

I exhale, slowly, and close my eyes.

In the darkness, all I see are the two crosses, ribbon tails dancing in the wind.

Another ten minutes passes before I get the nerve to approach Sanchez again. She's huddled around other officers, all of them staring at their devices.

"What is it?" I ask.

"I've just been sent the accident report from your husband's crash."

"And?"

"The other victim was an adult female. Christine Fields."

"I know," I say. Reliving the details doesn't get any easier.

I haven't heard her name in a long time. I remember reading it, once I summoned the strength to look at the sterile report printed in the local paper. Two lives watered down to no more than a few hundred words in print.

"After the accident, did you ever have contact with her family?"

"No. There weren't any survivors. No one was there to give me answers."

There was an immense sadness knowing the accident that night had taken two lives, but I was overwhelmed with my own grief. I hadn't worried about the other family affected, only assumed they were going through the same tremendous loss I was.

"I looked up her name once," Steven adds, and I am surprised to hear he was more invested in what happened than I was. "She wasn't local. I always wondered if she didn't know how to navigate the roads, and that's what caused the accident."

"I was going to ask about that. The report is very vague." Sanchez clears her throat. "Who caused the accident?"

I inhale sharply and turn. Piper sees that I'm struggling, and reaches out, but I step away from her. Steven, seeing my reaction, takes a step closer to the detective.

"It's not clear what happened. As Emma said, no one was around to see."

"I understand." The detective clears her throat again. "Christine Fields wasn't married at the time of her death. No children. I understand why seeing the memorial triggered your memory, but I'm not seeing any connection to what is happening now."

"Thank you, Detective," Steven says, turning to sit back on the sofa. Clearly, reliving the details of his brother's death has exhausted him. It's a night neither of us cares to think about.

"We'll be in here," Piper adds, "if you uncover anything else."

It's hard to tell whether she, or anyone else in the room, for that matter, believes this is a plausible scenario—David's accident somehow being connected to Claire's abduction.

I remain silent, my thoughts still hovering around the question Sanchez asked. *Who caused the accident?*

There was a reason David was on the road that night, a reason he was unfocused and distracted. My eyes cut over to Steven. For two years, he's believed David stormed out and sped away because of an argument they'd had. He's blamed himself for David's death, but it wasn't his fault.

It was mine.

FORTY-FIVE

THE NIGHT OF THE ACCIDENT

Life is ceremonial, filled with events to help escort us from one phase to the next. Graduations and birthdays. Weddings and anniversaries. Baby showers and parties. These are the moments people tend to revisit when life flashes before their eyes.

The smaller things are easily glossed over. Everyone remembers a first kiss, but rarely the second or the tenth or the hundredth. Happy moments, like a child losing a tooth or hitting a baseball for the first time.

And very few people talk about the mundane moments. The annoying sense of routine that sets in between all these monumental celebrations.

The missed alarms and traffic jams and unexpected expenses that color life dark, casting shadows on those shining moments we wish we could live in forever.

David and I had many shining moments, but like everyone else, we let the stressful moments get the best of us.

The day David died was a typical one. Of course, neither of us knew it would be his last, and perhaps if we did, it would have unfolded differently.

Claire was in the preschool program at North Ridge Elementary, and I'd returned to work full-time after taking an extended maternity leave to be with her during those early years. My reaction to our changing circumstances varied from day to day, like flipping a coin. I was happy to return to the classroom and I was resentful of the time I was spending away from home. I was excited for Claire to enter a new phase of her life and I was mourning how quickly the years already seemed to be passing.

David, too, was settling into a new routine. Having us both out of the house more gave him time to take on new projects at work. For the first time since Claire was born, he was also returning to music.

"Do you remember that band that was playing at The Sugar Shack last summer?" he asked me that morning. "We saw them that night we hired a sitter."

We were in the kitchen. Claire sat at the table, shoveling scoops of oatmeal into her mouth. I was standing behind her, trying to smooth her tangled hair into a braid. Another rushed morning, another moment taken for granted. My overwhelming irritation that David was talking to me about some band as I was trying to get us all out the door.

"Yeah, I guess."

"I told you I went to school with the bass player, remember?"

The elastic band in my hand snapped against my skin, and Claire squealed. I sighed, "Spit it out, David."

David smiled. "He messaged me last night and said their guitar player quit. He wanted to know if I'd be interested in joining them for a few shows. See how it goes."

I laughed, but the sound was cruel. "Seriously? You're wanting to join a band?"

"I thought maybe we could talk about it—"

"Talk about it. When? In between school and work and

Claire's dance classes? Or the weekends, which you always have devoted to some little project?"

"I know our lives are busy, but I've not played with another group since before Claire was born."

"Grab your backpack," I told Claire. "I'll meet you in the car."

She obeyed, stopping only to give David a hug. He kissed the top of her forehead and said he loved her. He waited until she'd gone outside before continuing the conversation.

"I think this would be good for me," he said.

"What about what's good for me? Our lives are busy enough as it is. And you're not the only one who has sacrificed. Why do you think I haven't painted since Claire was born? Silly hobbies are no longer a priority."

"I think it would be good for you to paint again, just like I would like to play music. We're parents now. We're older, sure. But we can still make time for us."

He stepped closer, pulling me into an embrace, but I pushed him away.

"There's never enough time, don't you see that? Even now I'm running late."

"I wasn't trying to upset you."

But his suggestion *had* upset me. His perceived selfishness. I'd stretched myself so thin, and all he wanted to do was pull on my edges a little more.

"We'll talk about this later," I said, as I rushed out the door.

"Sure. I'll see you tonight at Steven's."

"What?"

"We're having dinner there tonight. He invited us last week."

"I thought he was in Chicago."

"That's next week," David said. "He wanted to see us before he left."

I hurried out to the car, frustrated I'd forgotten.

Routine. It was the only thing that kept our world spinning, and I was so devoted to it, I barely thought about my argument with David. Perhaps, if I'd thought more about it, I would have called him to apologize for snapping. It was something that had started happening more often, a byproduct of the stressful moments that kept accumulating, like dark clouds in the sky above.

It started raining that day at noon and didn't stop. I can remember looking out the window of my classroom, amazed at how quickly the clear blue sky had turned dangerous and gray. There had even been rumors we might release students early, before the storm set in, but that didn't happen. Claire and I skipped to my car after school, huddled beneath an umbrella, and made it home just in time to get a little homework done before heading to Steven's house.

Steven wasn't there when we arrived. He sent a message apologizing for being late, provided us the code to enter the house. Claire and I went inside and passed the time playing reading games on my phone. Thirty minutes later, David showed up, but there was still no sign of Steven.

"Where is he?" he asked, looking around the house as though his brother might spontaneously appear.

"He said he was late. Something to do with work."

I kept my answers short, still irritated from our fight that morning. David was still annoyed too, started calling his brother nonstop.

When Steven finally arrived, you could smell the alcohol on him. He stumbled inside, all smiles and jokes, asking Claire what she'd like to cook for dinner, a meal we should have already finished by then.

"Can I talk to you for a minute?" David said to his brother, irritated.

"I'll take Claire downstairs," I said. "Show her the music room."

There we were, in Steven's massive basement, Claire crawling around on the rug. I was worried about her breaking something David and I could never afford to fix. I began singing, trying to drown out the voices from upstairs, which were only getting louder, angrier.

Then I saw the look on David's face when he came down the staircase. I saw his hurt and suffering, but instead of feeling empathy, I was cross.

"How did that go?" I asked.

"About as you'd expect. Steven thinks he's done nothing wrong. Says I'm the one being selfish for ruining his invitation for dinner." He picked Claire up and gave her a tight hug. "I told him we might stay away until he can get his act together."

"Are you sure that's what is really bothering you?"

He looked perplexed, gently putting Claire on the couch beside me. "What do you mean?"

"I keep going over our conversation this morning. You wanting to join a *band*."

"What does any of that have to do with Steven?"

"Maybe instead of picking a fight with your brother you should just admit the truth. That you're jealous of him."

He ran his hands through his hair, exhaled. "I don't know where this is coming from. I'm not jealous of Steven."

"*Steven* can join a band. Go out drinking with the guys. Travel the world. Have a late dinner on a school night and not think twice about any of it."

"I wasn't trying to start an argument this morning. I was only saying we could both make time to do things we enjoy." He sat beside me then. "Let's just go home. We can cook something easy, maybe share a glass of wine and talk before bed. Just the two of us."

But I was angry and didn't feel like reconciling so easily. "Go ahead. Claire and I will pick up takeout."

I watched as David grabbed his car keys and stormed off.

Back home, the clock above the fireplace rang at nine o'clock. David should have made it home before me, but then I thought about our argument. Maybe he was driving around, allowing his anger to simmer. I took out my phone and called him, but it went straight to voicemail: *You've reached David. Or rather, you* haven't *reached David. Leave a message and I'll call you back.*

A rumble of thunder tore through the silence, even seemed to shake the house. The storm. Could it be messing with the cell phone signal? Or maybe, David was more upset about our argument than I realized. He could have decided to drive back to Steven's house or meet one of his co-workers at The Sugar Shack for a drink. Maybe he was avoiding me.

Another thirty minutes passed before I started to really worry. Even if David was angry, he wouldn't want this. He wouldn't want me staying up, wondering where he was.

I was elated when I heard the sound of a car door slamming outside. I jumped off the couch, rushed to the front door. My arms were outstretched, ready for a hug, an apology sitting on my tongue.

But when I opened the front door, it wasn't David I saw. The face was hard to see; the bursts of red and blue lights hurt my eyes.

"Are you Emma Howard?" the police officer asked. I'd been able to figure out that much, but I still didn't understand why he was here. Rather, I dreaded why he was here. My body tensed up as I prepared for the words I never wanted to hear him say.

The words came, accompanied by a guilt and grief and sadness that have never left.

A car accident. A stoplight was damaged in the storm, which caused a traffic jam on the highway. That's why David had decided to cut through the cornfields, taking the backroads that would lead to our house.

The storm was peaking, and somehow— still no one is sure how—the two cars collided and both drivers died. I couldn't figure out why David was on the road so late in the first place. Even if he'd decided to meet friends at the bar, he never would have had a couple drinks and then gotten behind the wheel, especially in a storm.

It would have been so much easier to blame the weather or the other driver or his brother, and, quietly, I suppose that's what I did.

It wasn't until a few days after the crash, when they'd released his vehicle from the impound lot, that I realized why he was late.

After our fight, he'd driven across town to an arts and craft store, the one we frequented back when we were dating. He'd bought me some fresh canvases and paints and brushes. He even bought an art book, something to ease me back into painting. The receipt was still in the bag, proving it was the last place he'd stopped before starting to drive home.

While I'd been angry with him, preoccupied with my own responsibilities, David had been thinking about me. He wasn't venting to his brother or releasing steam at the bar. He was only doing what he'd always done: trying to make me happy.

That argument in Steven's basement began playing on a loop, and it was all I could do not to scream. I would have given anything to be able to rewind the hours and days, go back to that moment. I should have savored that last morning together, that last night, not rushed us out the door. I should have considered what he needed to make him happy, not been consumed with my own wants.

But I didn't. I wasted our last moments together. I wasted the love he'd always made a priority. Even then, on that last day,

David put me first, and it was that selflessness that put him on the road in the car at the exact moment when his life ended.

I took him for granted, a realization I'm forced to live with for the rest of my life.

FORTY-SIX

There's a sinking feeling in my chest. Guilt rises, hot and heavy, and it takes all the strength I have to swallow it down so no one will see.

Everyone who talks about David always comments on how loving our relationship was, how they'd never known a happier couple.

If only those same people knew I'd squandered our final moments together. If only those same people knew the only reason David was on the road that night is that he was trying to appease me, a near impossible task.

Most days, I'd like to think our marriage was strong. I'd like to think David was happy. But his death taught me that it only took one weak moment to upend the perfect life we'd created together. At least, I thought I'd learned my lesson.

If I had, I wouldn't have let Claire out of my sight. I would have guarded her in the same way I should have protected David's heart.

I didn't. And now they're both gone.

Across the room, I see Piper and Steven sitting on the couch. They're talking quietly. Steven wraps his arms around her, pulling her in for a hug. I'm jealous of their relationship and the years they still have together. Years that David and I will never have again.

But I'm also ashamed that my actions that day took David away from his brother and his daughter and everyone else who ever loved him. Would they ever be able to forgive me if they knew the truth?

I don't believe they would, which is why I have avoided David's family as much as possible in the years since his death. It's painful being around them, watching my own sadness reflected in them. But I'm also overwhelmed by the knowledge that everything that happened was my fault. Steven thinks he is to blame, but he doesn't know about our second argument. He doesn't know David stormed out of the house because of me.

My selfishness that day cost me my husband. My selfishness in the years that followed prevented me from seeing the other loss that night. Christine Fields.

Sanchez has promised to let me know if she uncovers anything important, but I'm sick of sitting in this room and waiting. It feels like the walls are collapsing around me, preventing me from seeing the bigger picture.

"I need some air," I say, standing and walking toward the porch door.

"You need some company?" Piper asks.

"No. I want to be alone."

Before I leave the room, Piper and Steven share a look. They are trying to be helpful and have provided far more comfort than I ever would have guessed before this night. But right now, I don't need the background noise of family or friends or the police. I need to be alone. I need to think.

Sure, Sanchez has access to police records, but those can be limited when giving you the full idea of a person. Much like the accident report in the paper, and the obituary that followed, it's based too much on facts, leaving out the shining moments that make a person who they really are.

There was no mention of David's love of music, his devotion to his daughter and family, how even in his last moments of life, he was consumed with trying to make others happy.

If all these details were omitted from David's story, there must be details about Christine Fields's life too that were overlooked, information Sanchez isn't likely to uncover in a database.

I turn to the universal almanac of life: social media.

After years of trying to avoid it, the name Christine Fields now sits at the forefront of my mind. I feel a sudden need to know more about her. Maybe it's because I have very little good in my own life. Isn't that what we do to distract us? We relish in reality television, town gossip, even random Facebook drama between strangers, anything that puts other people's problems in the spotlight, leaving our own faults unseen in the shadows.

The name Christine Fields is fairly common. As I type her name into the search engine, I'm not confident how easy it will be to find any information at all.

Steven had said she was from Whitaker, only a couple hours south from here. That location will have to be specific enough. I don't even know what the woman looks like. I know the exact moment of her death, but nothing of her life.

A handful of Christine Fields appear on the page. The list narrows when I type in her location. And then I see it, a memorial page dedicated to Christine Abigail Fields, who died in 2020 at the age of twenty-nine.

Her bright smile fills the screen. Blonde hair. Brown eyes. Her hair is styled in soft curls, falling in front of her face perfectly. She's wearing what looks like a bridesmaid's dress, a picture from another joyous ceremony in another person's life.

Another wave of guilt breaks. There's a reason I never did this in the years following David's death. It's simply too painful.

Having one death on my conscience is bad enough, let alone two.

The comments tend to revisit happy memories. Old classmates telling funny stories about their school days. A cousin posting a picture of Christine when she was a child, her hair plaited and her mouth missing random teeth.

Apparently, like me, Christine was a teacher in the Whitaker area. There are even some comments left by the parents of former students.

We'll miss you, Ms. Fields.

More pictures fill up the feed, and I have a strong urge to shut off my phone and throw it across the damp yard. Still, I keep scrolling. Maybe this is what I deserve: to feel the full brunt of my actions that night, finally be aware of all the pain I caused.

As I come closer to the end of the page, another post captures my attention. In fact, it's the first one that was ever posted. It reads:

In loving memory of Christine Fields. A daughter. A sister. A teacher. Until we meet again, my love.

The post was created by a man named Jonathan Archer. I click on his profile, but it's set to private, and the profile picture is an avatar. Perhaps, like me, Jonathan Archer is using his grief as a shield, finding it safer to live behind it.

The pain and suffering I feel now over the loss of Claire mimics what Christine Fields's loved ones have felt in the past two years.

I click back to the original post. Beneath the words is a photo album. I begin scrolling. Some of the pictures I've already seen in previous posts, like the one of Christine as a bridesmaid in what I'm guessing was her sister's wedding.

I zoom in on that picture again, wanting to get a better look at her face, of all the faces of the people who were close to her, the faces of people who lost someone that night like I lost David.

One of the faces stops me mid-thought, mid-breath. A warmth climbs my neck, resting around the base of my head. Without thinking I'm marching back into the house, straight to the living room, the phone in front of me, as though it's a staff guiding my path.

My voice, when I do speak, is so forceful, it grabs everyone's attention.

"Piper," I cry. "How do you know Christine Fields?"

FORTY-SEVEN

There's an anger rising inside me as I wait for an answer. Waiting and waiting. I can't do it anymore. The prize I've fought tooth and nail to find is right in front of me, just within reach, and I'm clawing at it.

I take a step closer to Piper, my voice raised, and repeat the question. "How do you know Christine Fields?"

"What's going on here?" Sanchez says, but I ignore her, my vision focused on Piper.

"I was right, wasn't I? Whoever took Claire has a connection to Christine. And you're here."

"Emma, I can explain."

I shove her. "Tell me where my daughter is."

"Emma, wait," Steven interjects. "Calm down."

"She knows Christine. She took Claire. Is that why you brought up the break-in? So you could make Steven look like he was the guilty party, when all along it was you?"

"Enough." Steven's anger, briefly, outweighs mine. The sheer weight of his voice makes me stop talking. "You can't come in here and start making accusations. You need to explain yourself."

I take a breath and look back at my phone, holding it up for them all to see.

"I found a memorial page for Christine Fields, the woman who died in David's accident. Piper knew her. Well, from the looks of it."

Tears sit in the corner of Piper's eyes. Her hand is covering her mouth. I think of the strange reaction she had earlier tonight when she drove me to the memorial. Refusing to get out of the car. She wasn't afraid or worried I was unstable. She was just as bothered by the place as I was; it's where she lost her friend.

Steven takes the phone, gets a better look at the picture. "I'm sure there's an explanation for this." But his voice is wavering. He looks to his wife. "Tell us what's going on."

Her voice trembles. "I knew Christine, but that doesn't mean I did anything to Claire."

"What are the odds your friend and my husband died and you're the only connection between us? Is that why you're here, why you married into the family in the first place? Is this all some kind of sick revenge?" I look to Steven. "Did you even know she knew that woman?"

"No, I didn't." His voice is unsteady, trying to remain true to his wife and keep his bearings all at the same time. "Piper, you need to start talking."

"Can we have a minute? Just the two of us?" she asks her husband.

"I'm not going anywhere," I say.

"I'll stay too," Sanchez says. Is she suspicious of Piper now? Curious about the connection? Or is she afraid of what might happen if she leaves me alone with my sister-in-law?

Piper sits on the couch. She takes several deep breaths before she begins.

"Yes, I knew Christine. I mean, I didn't just *know* her. We were roommates in college. She was like a sister to me."

"That's why you did this. You blame me or David or both—"

"Emma, stop," Steven says, holding me back. He looks at his wife, nervously. "Go on."

"When Christine died, I was devastated. It was so sudden and unexpected. Both of you know what it's like. And yes, when I first reached out to you, it was because I wanted to know more about David. I was still grieving myself, trying to find a way to move forward without my best friend. I just felt like I needed more. I needed to understand what had happened. Why it happened. And trying to blame the other driver was the only way I could make sense of it."

She looks at Steven. "But then I met you, and all those feelings just went away. I was immediately interested in you. An hour into our conversation, and I'd completely forgotten about David. You were the one I wanted to know."

"Why didn't you ever tell me?"

"Because I didn't want you to think what you're thinking right now. That I only tracked you down because of the accident. Sure, that's why I first sought you out, but that's not the reason I stayed. This isn't about revenge or justice. I fell in love with you."

Steven seems to soften, but fresh anger continues writhing inside of me. "I don't believe you," I say.

She addresses me now. "And then I met you and Claire. Any irrational anger I had at David or the world went away. I realized the accident was no one's fault."

My throat feels raw, like I'm about to cry. I look away so she can't see.

"All the times I talked to you about David," Steven says. "You never told me."

"I thought it was better for you to vent than to let you know. I realized I didn't have to talk about Christine. We were processing our grief at the same time in different ways, even if you didn't know it.

"I'm sorry I didn't tell you and I'm sorry you had to find out now, like this. But even though I knew Christine, I would never do anything to hurt Claire. All I want is to help bring her back. That's why I brought up the break-in. And I'll come clean about Christine and anything else if it means Claire is safe."

It's hard for me to know what to think. My loyalties tonight have already been tested. First, with my trust in Laura, then again with Sarah and her multiple betrayals.

"You say you're not involved in Claire's disappearance. That you only want to help."

"Yes, Emma. I promise."

I sit in the chair across from her, my frame and posture almost matching hers.

"Then let's start with you telling me about the other people in Christine's life. If one of them is out for revenge, odds are you know them."

FORTY-EIGHT

Tensions have settled, prompting Sanchez to go back outside and continue discussing the investigation. It's clear she doesn't think this connection will bring us closer to finding Claire, and now that she's no longer worried I'll deck my sister-in-law, she has left the three of us alone.

There's still a biting sense of betrayal that Piper knew Christine and never told me—never told her own husband— that there was this grave connection bringing us together and none of us knew it. But we've explored all possible avenues for finding Claire in the present: the surveillance tapes, the fake ransom, the rental car. Perhaps the trail leading back to her isn't clearly set. Perhaps the key to finding her remains in the past.

"Christine was a good person. Just the best. We grew up together back in Whitaker and were roommates in college. She was a teacher, like you. She actually reminds me of you in many ways." She smiles a sad smile. "It's funny that two people who never met can remind you so much of each other. You would have liked her."

I can't focus on the loss of Christine. Or David. The sadness is too much. I need to focus on the facts, anything that could lead me toward Claire.

"What about her family? Would any of them take Claire as a way to punish me for what happened to Christine?"

"No. Her family are good people. Of course, they were devastated when she died. We all were. But they would never do anything like this."

"You said they're not from here, but someone must have cared enough about Christine to put up that memorial."

"It's common for people to do that in the spot where the person died," Steven adds.

"Yes, but Christine wasn't from here. She was from Whitaker." I look to Christine. "Does she have any family in the area?"

"No. Not any that I know." She pauses. "I'm the only person here who knows her."

It's that coincidence that still bothers me. Piper appears to be helpful, but she could still have an axe to grind. She might only be playing the part of the grieving friend now to cover her tracks.

"You didn't move here until after the accident," Steven says. "If Christine didn't have a connection to this town, why was she here that night?"

"It's complicated." Piper suddenly seems conflicted about sharing her friend's secrets. "She was considering moving here."

"But why? There has to be a reason she was considering starting her life over."

"She was getting out of a bad relationship."

"Jonathan Archer," I say. I remember seeing his name on the memorial Facebook post.

Piper's eyes go wide. "Yeah. How did you know?"

"He posted on the website. It looks like he might have even created it."

Piper rolls her eyes, wiping beneath them. "Oh yeah, I'm sure. He wouldn't let Christine rest. Even after she died."

"The relationship was that bad?" Steven asks.

"You have no idea. They started dating in college. Continued dating after he dropped out, and he was like this huge weight Christine carried around all the time. He constantly brought her down."

"Was he violent?" I ask.

"Not physically. But the way he controlled her... it was borderline abusive. We tried to get her to leave him for years." Another wave of emotion rises, and she begins to cry. "That's what upset me the most when she died. She was finally starting to live life on her own terms, and then it was all over."

"Do you think this ex-boyfriend could be involved?"

"I've no idea. For all I know, he's still bumming off people back in Whitaker. I was happy to never talk to him again."

"But if he was abusive, controlling. That sounds like the type of person who might be capable of kidnapping a child."

"He doesn't have the brains for that sort of thing. The guy couldn't follow through with one thing his entire life. I'm sorry, Emma. But I really don't think there is a connection between the accident and what's happening with Claire now."

"But the memorial. The ribbon. It represents a missing a child. We all know a child wasn't killed, so the only thing that could be referring to is Claire."

Piper gasps and her jaw drops, as though the final piece of the puzzle is falling into place.

"Oh my gosh," she says.

"What is it?"

"It can't be... I mean, no one else knew."

"Piper, what is it?"

"Christine was pregnant. That's what gave her the nerve to finally leave Jonathan. That's why she was moving here, to start a new life for her and the baby. Without him."

That's it. The missing link we've been trying to find. I stand, my excitement overflowing.

"That's what the ribbon represents. A child did die that night. There were only two crosses. One of the crosses doesn't signify David. It represents Christine and her child."

"But I'm telling you. No one knew. She didn't tell her parents or her sister. Only me. She didn't want anyone else to know until she was settled somewhere safe. She was afraid if Jonathan found out, he'd keep her from leaving."

"Did you tell anyone after she died?" Steven asks.

"No," Piper says. "Her family was already devastated. I didn't want to add more sadness."

"Maybe someone else found out after she died? Did they perform an autopsy or something? They could have found out she was pregnant that way."

"Sanchez didn't say anything about a pregnancy in the report. It's my understanding they only perform a full autopsy if they're searching for cause of death. It was a car crash, so there may not have been a reason."

"But maybe he still found out. Whoever put the memorial there, they must have known about the pregnancy," I say. "You need to tell us everything you know about this Jonathan Archer. Tell the police. Maybe he has nothing to do with Claire's disappearance, but if he does, this might be the reason Claire was targeted. He's mourning the loss of Christine and his child. He put up the memorial. And now he's getting revenge."

"We've not had any contact since Christine died. Last I know, he was working at a gas station back in Whitaker."

"His Facebook profile is set to private." I look at my phone, useless. "Do you have a picture of him?"

"Let me see," she says, scrolling through the pictures on her phone. "I tried to avoid him when I could, but I've kept every picture I ever had of Christine. He's liable to be in one of them." After a few seconds, she stops scrolling and holds out her phone. "Here."

Christine is standing on the mountainside and there's a man

with one arm wrapped around her, the other arm outstretched in order to take the selfie.

I'm assuming the man is Jonathan Archer, but that's not the name I know him by.

The man standing beside Christine Fields in the picture is North Ridge Elementary's most eligible bachelor: Jack Fox.

FORTY-NINE

I feel bad about what happened to Dr. Meade.

I didn't have time to do anything with the body. Eventually, someone will find it. Someone will either start looking for her or looking for me. I hope they find it before she starts to stink. I carried it down the basement steps, put it in the same place where the girl had been.

Regardless of how things ended, I think Dr. Meade would be proud of what I've done. I've finally taken control of my own life, taken ownership of my mistakes. Before I met her, I was at my darkest point. Christine was gone, taking with her our child and any future I'd imagined we might have. I decided I couldn't live with the pain any longer. I took a handful of pills, washed it down with a fifth of whiskey, Dad's favorite brand, and waited for the end.

When I awoke in the hospital, I was told I'd have to stay for an undetermined amount of time, long enough for the doctors to be certain I wouldn't try hurting myself again. That's where I met Dr. Meade. For the first time since the accident, I opened up about Christine and the baby and all my pain. Dr. Meade listened, said she believed I could overcome it.

I tried it her way for a while. When I first moved to North Ridge, it was because of a pulling sensation to be closer to Christine. Her body may have been buried in Whitaker, but something about this place had called to her, brought her here for her final moments. And let's face it, I needed the change of scenery.

I took the job at North Ridge Elementary to feel closer to her. Spending the day as she would have spent it made me feel closer to her. Emma worked there, too. The only other person who could possibly understand my loss. Working alongside her seemed to make sense. As though our greatest losses had somehow brought us together.

Emma was someone I could model myself after. She was strong, positive, independent. She had to be all these things because her daughter, Claire, depended on her. Emma had also suffered a loss, maybe not as deep as mine, but seeing her persevere gave me the confidence I could do the same.

Of course, I didn't tell her about my history. Using my mother's maiden name—Fox—helped with that. In many ways, I started to feel like a different person. The type of man who was capable of taking control. I had a steady job for the first time in my life, a career that meant something, working alongside children, some of whom had the same challenges I did growing up.

Dr. Meade was so proud of me. I was proud of myself. For a while, I thought I could do it. Live this life. Be this person.

And then the one-year anniversary hit. I'd considered calling in sick that day. I'd thought I'd spend the afternoon in the cornfields, changing the flowers at the memorial site. But then I asked myself, what would Jack Fox do? Sure, Jonathan Archer would whine and cry the day away. But Jack? He would take charge. Push through. Be strong.

I'd made it through the first half of the day and barely thought about Christine. I was in my new life, living my new purpose. And then Anna and I found Emma.

She was alone in the room. The lights were off, the empty student desks in a semicircle, an audience of ghosts watching her despair. She wouldn't stop crying. She wouldn't stop talking about the past and that day. How hard her life was.

I knew in that moment I'd misunderstood her. She wasn't strong. She was weak. So weak, she didn't mind putting her grief on display for all her co-workers to see.

"Go home for the rest of the day," Ben had said. "Take some time to yourself."

No one could see the grimace on my face. The absolute disgust. Everyone making excuses for this woman, having no idea I was going through the exact same pain and keeping it all to myself. Couldn't Emma see it? That her life wasn't the only one that was ruined that night. Couldn't she understand how lucky she was to still have Claire? Her daughter. There were other people, like me, who had been left with nothing.

For weeks, I couldn't wipe the image of Emma crying from my mind. I wanted to grab her and shake her, curse her for taking all she had left for granted. When our co-workers treated her like everything was normal, I wanted to do the same to them. I fell back into my old thought patterns, thinking of my childhood and Christine and the accident. I felt the person I'd created—Jack Fox —slipping away.

It was around that time Dr. Meade said she was moving her practice. It felt like the one person who still knew me—the one person who actually appreciated me, flaws and all—was leaving.

I still made time to remember Christine and the baby every night, mourn the time that was taken from us, but the tribute no longer helped the way it once did. I was more aware than ever that I had nothing, all while there were people out there taking for granted everything they had.

That's when it first came to me: The Plan.

What I wanted more than anything was another chance at

my life with Christine. An opportunity to be a husband and a father. I could never get her back—no one would ever compare. But maybe, just maybe, I could take the little love I had left and give it to someone who needed it.

FIFTY

EMMA

Heat rises through my body, settling between my temples. When I speak it comes out in a gasp.

"This can't be right," I pant. "I know him."

"You know Jonathan?" Now Piper is pulling back at the phone, trying to get a glimpse, making sure we're talking about the same person.

"I don't know him as Jonathan. This is Jack. He works with me at the school."

Whatever wall that existed in Piper's mind preventing her from believing her friend's partner could be involved must crumble. The look on her face is one of shock and fear and... understanding. Her friend's controlling lover, the one she tried desperately to escape in the days leading up to her death, has taken Claire.

"You have to tell the police," she says, her voice urgent. "Now."

I rush outside, Piper and Steven fast behind me. When I find the detective, she's huddled around a trio of other officers.

"Sanchez, I need to show you something," I say, ramming myself into the circle.

"What is it?"

"The man in this picture took Claire. I know him," I say, holding out the phone for her to see. "He was in a relationship with Christine Fields."

"The woman from your husband's car accident?"

"Yes. But he goes by a different name now. Jack Fox. He works with me."

This detail perks her interest more than any of the others. "Does your daughter know him?"

"Yes. He's one of the assistants in our pod."

I recall the video evidence of Claire leaving the pumpkin patch, holding her abductor's hand. She didn't seem scared or in distress, and it's because she wasn't. Mr. Fox wasn't a stranger to her. He's a trusted teacher, her mother's friend. She wouldn't think twice about following his orders, especially if he convinced her I'd given her permission to leave with him.

There's no telling what he's done with her since they left.

"When's the last time you saw him?"

"Today. He was a chaperone on the field trip." For the first time since Claire was taken, my thoughts are coming together, creating an image both clear and disturbing. "And he was at the school tonight. Helping with the search."

"You saw him there?"

"No, but the other volunteers told me he was out helping."

"We need to talk to him," Sanchez says. "Find out if this is a coincidence or something more."

"I know it's him!"

I no longer believe anything about tonight is a coincidence. This entire event was planned. The rental car. Katy going missing. Her disappearance only served as a distraction. And she would have listened to Mr. Fox just as easily as Claire did. Jack orchestrated the chaos so he could take Claire away from me.

Sanchez is on the phone barking orders, and I'm trying my

best not to hyperventilate. I hold out the phone, staring at the picture once again.

"Emma." Steven is standing behind me, his hand placed gently on my shoulder. "Tell us what you know about this man."

"He's one of the two assistants that works with our grade level," I say. "He was at the pumpkin patch today. And he's been working at the school for more than a year. That's given him plenty of time to get to know me and—"

"And Claire." Steven finishes my sentence, slapping the phone back onto the table between us. He covers his face with his hands, struggles to breathe. "He lost his baby in the accident."

"And now he's trying to take mine." I turn to Piper. "You know him better than I do. The real him. Is he capable of hurting Claire?"

"I already told you. He was controlling and emotionally abusive." She presents these facts as an offering, though the hope in her words quickly fades. "But if he's really the one who took Claire, I can't say what he's capable of doing. It's possible losing Christine has pushed him over the edge."

"If he's spent the past year planning this..." Steven starts, but his words fall away. Nothing could make the situation any better. Clearly, Jack Fox isn't thinking with a rational mind.

Sanchez is still on the phone. It's difficult to tell whether any progress is being made. Is she trying to avoid looking at me? Maybe this isn't the lead I was hoping it was. Or maybe she already knows something I don't, something that could place Claire in even more danger.

I collapse into one of the chairs beside the table and hold my head in my hands. I've already lost David. I can't lose Claire, too.

The only other person who knows this pain—of what it's like to lose both a partner and a child—is Jack Fox. That must be what motivated him to take her in the first place. He wants me to feel the same agony he's been suffering for the past two years.

FIFTY-ONE

Piper, Steven and I make our way back into the living room to wait until someone presents us with more information. I almost leap out of my seat when Sanchez re-enters the room. Any hope I had quickly fades when I see the look on her face.

"Are you sure you saw Jack Fox on the field trip?"

"Yes. He was one of the chaperones."

"Did you see him leave?"

"No, but I didn't see most people leave. They'd been given permission to go before I returned from the corn maze." I think of the video, the swarms of people on the playground and near the gate. Then I imagine those people moving toward the parking lot. "No one was watching them."

"And you're sure he was at the school earlier this evening helping with the search?"

"Yes."

"I radioed over to the officers we have at the school. Fox isn't there now, and there's no word on when or if he left." She sounds disappointed. "We pulled his address and we're sending officers over there right now."

"Do you think he's the one who took Claire?" Steven asks.

"I'm not sure of anything yet," Sanchez says. "But it's suspicious that he has a connection to both Claire's abduction and the car accident. Even weirder that he's going around using two names." She looks at me now. "I need you to tell me everything you know about him."

I exhale and close my eyes, trying not to focus on what could be happening at this moment. Is Jack taking care of Claire? Is he hurting her? Where are they?

Instead, I try to focus on what I do know. At least, what he's revealed to me in the past year.

"He started working at the school last spring. As an assistant. He's in and out of all our rooms. He interacts with all the kids, including Claire."

"I'm confused about his role here," Sanchez says. "Is he, like, an extra teacher?"

"The school hires extra help for grades K-2. The assistants make copies, read with students one-on-one, escort them to and from their elective classes. Sometimes they'll cover classes for teachers while we're in a meeting. Jack said he was working on finishing his teaching degree, if that's even true. If he doesn't have a criminal record, nothing would stop him from getting the job."

"His background looks clean. It looks like he started going by his mother's maiden name, Fox, a little more than a year ago. There's nothing illegal about that," Sanchez says. "But it's suspicious if he changed his name to intentionally deceive you."

What is ironic, is that even if he'd gone by his given name, Jonathan Archer, I still wouldn't have made the connection. That's how little I had researched Christine Fields and her life.

"Do you think that's why he did it?"

"He made the change around the time he started working at the school," she says. "It would make sense if his plan was to get closer to you and Claire."

"Clearly he'd been planning this. He rented the car.

Brought a change of clothes. He made sure everyone was looking for Katy." Each evidence knocks into me like unforgiving waves. I struggle to catch my breath. It's becoming clear just how much I'm up against. "He did all this so he could take Claire."

"Stay calm," Piper says. She places her hands over mine. Her palm is cool to the touch.

"Keep focusing on Fox," Sanchez says. "Does he have any family here? Anyone who might be able to help us contact him?"

"He's been dating one of the other assistants at the school." The detail ramps up my excitement. "Her name is Anna. She was also at the pumpkin patch today."

"And did you see her at the school earlier tonight? Was she part of the search party?"

"Yes. I didn't see her, but Laura said she was out searching with the others."

"Let's work on tracking down Anna," Sanchez says. "If Fox did take Claire, he had to leave her alone long enough to return to the school. Maybe Anna is helping him."

I can't imagine Anna would do anything to hurt a child. As educators, our purpose revolves around protecting children. Building them up. Urging them to grow. We help them face challenges inside the classroom and try to instill tools that will help them once they return home. I can't imagine anyone in that position would ever want to hurt a child. Then again, an hour ago I would have thought the same thing about Jack.

I remind myself that Jack Fox is not who he pretends to be. He is not an educator. He is not a caretaker. And he's not a parent; no caring parent would wish this type of anguish on another person.

Jonathan Archer is a different man entirely. I know very little about him, other than he's a grieving man with little left to lose. If I want to bring Claire home, I need to figure out what he wants.

Sanchez's phone pings. Her eyes scan the message quickly, then she sighs.

"Officers are at his house now. There's no sign of him." She continues reading the message, and her expression changes.

"What is it?"

She takes a deep breath. "They've found a body."

FIFTY-TWO

Even though Dr. Meade is gone now, I'll never forget the lessons she taught me. She's the one who pushed me to create a new narrative, invent the person I wanted to be, instead of the grieving loser I really was.

For so long, my story was one of tragedy. Drunk father, absent mother. Underachiever. Weirdo. Freak. Then Christine came into my life, and none of those labels seemed to matter. Everything in my life prepared me for her, for the life we would build together.

I'd never committed to anything like I did Christine. She was beautiful and smart and confident... all the things I hoped to one day be. Having a woman like that allow me into her life was my greatest blessing, and I wouldn't take that for granted, squander that gift like my parents did.

No, what Christine and I had was rare and needed to be protected. That's why I went to such lengths to make her happy. I followed her to and from class to make sure she was safe. On nights when I was stuck working at the gas station, I'd message her every half hour to check she was okay.

I worried about Christine, that someone else would see how special she was and take advantage of her. Her friends, always urging her to go out on the weekends, never once considered how dangerous it could be. And don't even get me started on the men. They were enamored with her, like I was, but they didn't appreciate her. That's why whenever we went out together in public, at restaurants and bars and the movie theatre, I kept my arm around her, touching her at all times, so there wouldn't be any confusion about whether we were together.

Before she started teaching, she worked in a restaurant off-campus. The men there worried me the most, so I'd show up, stake out a booth in the corner, and watch her. When men would put their hands on her, pull her in for a conversation, it infuriated me. I caused a couple of scenes, and eventually she got fired, but I tried to make her see that it was a blessing in disguise. She didn't need that job or those men or her friends.

All she needed was me.

Our relationship wasn't always easy, but what thing worth having is? When Christine tried to pull away, I'd push harder. It was important that she understood how committed I was. That no matter what happened in life, I'd be there for her.

Still, I worried. When I was at work, she stopped responding to my text messages, allowing my calls to go to voicemail. She said she was asleep or sick. There always seemed to be some excuse why she couldn't talk to me. Then one night, I showed up to her apartment after work, but she wasn't there.

I'd made a copy of her key during our first week of dating. I didn't use it often—I didn't want her to feel violated—but I was so worried about her. I imagined her passed out on the floor, unable to call for help, and she needed someone like me to come in and save her. But when I went inside, the apartment was empty.

I searched every inch of that place, looking for any clue that would tell me where she went. Maybe she left me a note—it was so unlike Christine to keep secrets from me. I searched her drawers and closets, even the trash. And that's where I found it.

A pregnancy test. Christine was pregnant with my child. Our rare, precious love had created another life, and all her strange behavior in the past few weeks suddenly made sense. I called her, but she didn't answer at first, so I sent her a message:

I know about the baby. I'm so excited to start our lives together.

It was almost eight o'clock when she called me back.

She was emotional, unhinged. But that's a side effect of being pregnant, isn't it? She wanted to know how I'd found out. When I told her I was in her apartment, she was even more upset.

"Just tell me where you are," I told her. "I can find you and make everything better."

But she refused to tell me. She said she was driving around, trying to clear her head. She was crying harder and harder, and I couldn't figure out why she was so upset—and then the line went dead.

I tried calling her again, but the phone kept ringing. No answer.

It didn't matter. I knew she'd come home eventually. Now she needed me more than ever, so I waited, distracting myself with ideas of what our new life would be like together. I'd pick up extra shifts, get a new job if that's what needed to happen. I didn't want Christine to worry about teaching anymore. Her purpose was now to raise our child, and my job was to protect them both. I wouldn't throw away this gift. I wouldn't repeat the mistakes from my childhood. For two days, I remained in her apartment, sleeping in her bed, waiting for her to come home so we could start our new life together.

But when a person finally arrived, it wasn't Christine. It wasn't anyone I'd ever seen before. A local police officer caught *off guard to see that someone was home. And that's when she'd told me what happened in a town called North Ridge, a place we'd visited once in the early days of our relationship.*

She told me about the car accident. That Christine and the baby were...

A car horn blares. The car is veering off the side of the road. I turn the wheel, correcting myself just in time, but it was close. In the back seat, Claire begins to stir.

"Hush now, little girl," I coo. "Not much longer now."

Dr. Meade would be so disappointed in me. I'm falling back into negative thought patterns, focusing too much on the past instead of all the promise that is yet to come. I can't afford to make any more mistakes. Not when I'm this close—we're this close—to having everything we both deserve.

It's time for Step Three: Start Over.

Another couple of days of hiding out, waiting for the dust to settle, and I'll be home free. Right now, the disappearance of Claire is all over the news, but that story will soon be replaced by another one. And then another one. If life has taught me anything, it's that there's always a new tragedy just around the corner.

I turn on my blinker and pull off the highway.

FIFTY-THREE

EMMA

Sanchez has told the remaining officers at the school to be on the lookout for Jack and Anna. She sent another group of officers to Anna's house. This is the most concrete lead we've had since Claire was taken.

And yet all I can think about is what Sanchez said they discovered at the house:

They found a body.

"You have to tell me something," I beg her. "Go over there yourself, if you have to. I need to know if they've found Claire. I need to know if she's okay."

"Let me make a call."

She's waiting on information, too, and it's clear she's nervous. I'd been so relieved to make the connection between Jonathan Archer and Jack Fox, but none of that will matter if Claire is already dead.

Sanchez returns a few minutes later. "The body is an adult female. It's not Claire."

I exhale in relief, but then feel overwhelming guilt. I'm celebrating the fact that Claire wasn't the body found at Jack's

house, but someone else has still died. There's nothing to cele-
brate about that.

"Who is it they found at his house?"

"We don't have confirmation yet." She pauses. "Didn't you
say he was in a romantic relationship with one of the women at
the school?"

"Oh my gosh, Anna."

She'd been right beside me most of the day. I think of the
way she was talking about Jack, blushing at the sight of him and
smiling every time someone mentioned his name.

"I'm going to call her," I say, unlocking the screen of my
phone.

"Don't do that." Sanchez moves closer, as though she has
plans to physically stop me.

"Why? If we're trying to find Jack, we should be talking to
Anna. The two of them are close."

"But how close? How do you know she isn't helping him?
She could be an accomplice."

"Anna is my friend. She would never go along with a plan
that could endanger Claire."

"Sarah was also your friend," Piper says, her voice a
whisper.

My jaw clenches and I grind my teeth. I'd temporarily
forgotten about Sarah's role in all of this. Her betrayal is biting.
Because of her, Jack was provided the small window he needed
to snatch Claire. However, despite my anger, I know she never
intended for that to happen. If she'd had an inkling someone
was targeting my daughter, Sarah would do whatever necessary
to stop it from happening. And even Sanchez said Darren had
acted alone with the ransom attempt.

"Sarah made a mistake," I say, at last. "That's different from
someone deliberately doing something that would harm Claire."

"Sarah isn't the only person who lied," Sanchez reminds
me. "An hour ago, you didn't suspect Fox was involved either."

"Jack isn't who he pretended to be. Jonathan Archer has motive. He's connected to us through the car accident that killed David and Christine," I say. "Anna doesn't have any reason to go along with his plan. She would never hurt Claire, and if she had any idea that Jack did, she would turn him in."

From the moment she arrived on the scene, Sanchez has appeared calm and focused. Now, I'm noticing she seems hesitant. Her stare bounces between her watch and her phone.

"Just let me call her. Find out where she is," I beg. "She doesn't have a reason to think I'm onto her. Or Jack. She might be able to give us something useful."

"Okay. Let's go into one of these rooms." She turns on her heels, instructing the officers to remain quiet. Then she turns her attention to Piper and Steven. "You two stay out here."

Steven nods. He reaches out his arm, placing his hand on my shoulder. "Good luck."

We walk back into the music room, the closest location quiet enough for an important conversation to take place. It's already been the setting for many heart-to-hearts tonight, and I'm gearing up for another. In some ways, this phone call is more nerve-wracking than the ransom call. In that situation, I was at a total loss. Now, I'm closer than ever to finding out what happened to Claire. All I need is for Anna to give me information.

Whether she's still my friend, or as Sanchez has suggested, an enemy, is still unclear.

"Don't tell her our theories," Sanchez says. "Only try to figure out her location. And, if you can, find out Jack's whereabouts. But you don't need to mention him by name. You follow her lead. If she is involved, we don't want her getting suspicious."

I nod along, understanding Sanchez's logic, even if I don't agree. Anna wouldn't be involved. I'm certain of that.

I pull out my phone and pull up my contacts, clicking on

her name. I place the call on speaker, holding the device between us, like a candle in the dark.

There are three rings, and then an answer.

"Emma? Is that you?"

It's Anna's voice. At least the body they found at the house doesn't belong to her. There's a distracting background sound bleeding into the call.

"Yes. It's me," I say. "Where are you? Are you still at the school?"

"I'm out in the fields," she says, which explains the noise. The more I listen, the more it sounds like wind and rain. "Have you heard anything about Claire?"

I look at Sanchez and she shakes her head, slightly.

"No. No. We still haven't found her."

"Dear God. I can't believe this is happening. I wanted to reach out to you, see how you were doing, but I figured you had enough on your mind."

"Yeah, I do." Nervousness is starting to creep into my words, and I'm afraid Anna will notice. "Where are you exactly? Are you with a search party?"

"No. I mean, I was. Our group has gotten smaller as night set in," she says. "But don't worry. There are still plenty of people out searching. I'm leaving now to grab some dinner. I told Ben and some of the others I'd meet them back here in the morning, if we haven't heard anything by then."

"So, there's no one out there with you?"

"We're about a mile away from the pumpkin patch, searching the woods behind the old library. The others pulled off before I realized my tire is flat. I'm stranded."

"They just left you there by yourself?"

"Please, don't worry about me. I'm close to a gas station. I can walk, if I have to. I'm trying to get a hold of Jack, but he—"

"Jack was with you?" The mention of his name excites me, and I cut her off. Sanchez gives me a warning look.

"He was. He left over an hour ago. He was running by the school to drop off supplies, then he was picking up dinner. I don't think any of us have eaten today."

"So, you've not seen him for an hour? Or more?"

"Yes." She is hesitant. "But don't worry. We're not the only group out here. There are others searching all over."

"Did Jack say anything about where he was going? If he was meeting with anyone else?"

Sanchez squeezes my forearm, a warning not to push.

"No," Anna says. "He just told me to finish up with the group and meet him at his house."

But we know Jack isn't at his house. The police are there, and a dead body, but not him. Could he have tampered with her tires?

"Anna, I need you to promise me something. If you hear from Jack, you need to call me immediately."

Sanchez squeezes my arm again, signals I should hang up the phone.

"Emma, why do you keep asking about Jack? You're worrying me."

Hang up now, Sanchez mouths. The intensity in her eyes worries me.

"Just promise me," I say, and I click off the line before Anna has a chance to respond.

"You were supposed to let her do the talking," Sanchez says. "You weren't supposed to make her think we were looking into Jack."

"I was trying to get as much information as possible," I say. "At least we know how far of a head start he has if he is making a run for it."

"Yeah, we figured that out." Her look sours. "But if Anna is helping him, then you've just given him a heads-up. He'll know we're onto him."

My gut tells me to trust Anna, but how many times have I

already been blindsided tonight? Sarah and Darren and Piper. Jack. I have no way of knowing whether Anna would remain loyal to him or me. My chest aches with anxiety and worry, as I realize what I've done.

Sanchez is right. I might have just ruined the last chance I had to get my daughter back.

FIFTY-FOUR

I'm only a few steps behind Sanchez. She stomps out of the room, immediately grabbing the attention of another officer.

"We need to send a car to the area behind the old library," she orders.

Steven appears at her side. "Did you find something?"

She keeps her attention on the officer, ignoring Steven's question. "The woman we're looking for is named Anna. She says her car has been tampered with. You need to let me know the minute we have eyes on her. And if you don't find her there, tell me that, too."

"Emma," Piper says, standing at my side. "What happened? Did Anna say anything?"

I close my eyes and pinch my temples, trying to recall her exact words. "She was leaving one of the search sites. She said Jack was with her up until an hour ago. Now, we don't know where he is."

"Why does Sanchez seem so upset?" Steven asks, his voice lowered.

But Sanchez hears him, and when she addresses the three of us, she doesn't hold back.

"I'm mad at myself for letting her call in the first place. It was a stupid choice. And now I'm worried that she might have tipped off the accomplice of our most-promising suspect."

"I... I didn't mean to do that."

"But you did. This is why we don't need your involvement. It's too personal. If you want to get your daughter back, the three of you need to stay out of our way." With an almost sing-song quality to her voice, she restates what she's said countless times this night. "We'll come to you when we have information."

With that, she storms out of the house, leaving us alone with a handful of officers. I walk into the living room and sit on the sofa. It isn't long before Steven and Piper join me.

"Did something go wrong?" Piper asks.

"I don't know. I wasn't trying to mess anything up. Sanchez thought I was asking too many questions about Jack, but all I was trying to do was gather information."

"Do you think it's possible Anna is helping him?" Steven sounds worried, like there might be some truth to Sanchez's theory.

"No. I don't think she would."

I know she wouldn't do anything to harm Claire. Or any child. I watch Anna interact with children every day at work. She has more patience than most of the teachers in the building. If she thought, even for a second, that one of our students was in danger, she'd act. She certainly wouldn't be a co-conspirator. Even her feelings for Jack wouldn't muddy her stance on protecting kids.

"The detectives don't know who to trust," Steven says. "They assume everyone has something to hide. Even us."

"I'm okay with that, as long as it leads us to Jack."

But I'm starting to worry that might not happen. According to Anna, no one has laid eyes on him in over an hour. What has he been doing during that time? Is he with Claire, or is she alone somewhere, scared and crying? Maybe he's leaving town. If that's the case, he's had a big enough head start that he could be anywhere.

What exactly is Jack's aim in all of this? Is he trying to punish me? I understand now that he lost his family in the same accident that killed David, so he must know I've already been punished. I lost my husband. Maybe he wants me to experience what he has felt in the past two years, what it is like to be totally and completely alone. Or maybe he's trying to piece his family back together; he lost a child, and now he has taken another.

There's a reason he accepted the job at North Ridge Elementary and used a different name. He's been trying to avoid detection from the start, which means he's had over a year to plan. He could have accessed new identification cards and passports with the intention of starting over somewhere new, raising Claire as his own. I've read stories about that before. The victims become so traumatized they eventually go along with their new life, forget about the one they left behind.

Or could his purpose be more violent? A murder-suicide, maybe, leaving me alone to feel the full brunt of his actions.

Whatever his plan, I may never be able to bring my daughter home.

My phone rings again. When I glance at the screen, it's Anna calling back.

Instinctively, I look in the direction where Sanchez has stood most of the night, but she isn't there. She's outside, doing her best to avoid me.

"Who is it?" Piper asks.

"It's Anna." I look at them, the phone vibrating in my hand. "Should I answer?"

They look equally conflicted. The only reason to trust Anna is based on my gut. What if Sanchez is right, and Anna is a part of this?

Finally, Steven nods, his eyes darting in the direction of the music room. "Answer it."

I bring the phone to my ear. "Anna?"

"Emma, thank God. What is going on?"

"I don't know. Where are you?"

"An officer showed up and gave me a ride to the police station. They said they want to talk to me."

I'm nervous. If this was true, would Anna still have access to her phone? Maybe there isn't reason to consider her a suspect, and the police are just keeping tabs on her, for her own safety. I take Sanchez's advice, letting her lead the conversation.

"What did they say exactly?"

"They were asking questions about Jack. They seemed a little less... intense once they saw that my tires were slashed, but I'm still so confused." She pauses. "The police don't actually think Jack is involved with Claire's disappearance, do they?"

I'm so afraid of saying the wrong thing. I wish I hadn't answered the call at all. This is putting me dangerously close to what could be the kidnapper's accomplice.

"I don't know. They aren't telling me much anymore," I answer, honestly.

There's a long silence, and I'm afraid of what Anna will say next. If she is working with Jack, she could end the call and let him know the police are onto him.

"Emma, there's something I need to tell you," she says. "Something that has been bothering me all night."

"What is it? Is it about Claire?"

"No. It's about Jack." She pauses again. "When word started to circulate that Claire was missing, all of us were shocked. When we decided to head to the school, I called Jack and told him. He didn't want to come at first, but eventually he did.

"At the school, the officers started asking us questions about the field trip, especially people who had been there that day.

They wanted to know what time we arrived. What we'd seen. When we'd left.

"I overheard the police talking to Jack. They were asking him the same questions they asked me and everyone else. He told the officer he left the pumpkin patch the same time I did. But he didn't. Jack left before." She sounds worried, almost defensive. "I just thought we were all under stress and tired. Maybe he forgot that detail. But now, the questions you're asking me... it makes me wonder if he lied on purpose."

"The officer he spoke with... did you get his name?"

"No. There were so many of them walking around. And that's something else. All those cops seemed to bother Jack. I mean, we were all worried. But Jack... he seemed scared."

"My goodness."

"I should have said something earlier, but I didn't really think it meant anything, until I got your phone call and the police showed up."

"Anna, has Jack ever mentioned the name Jonathan Archer to you?"

"No. Who is that?"

I can hear it in her voice. She's clueless. And scared.

"That's Jack's real name. I'm still not sure of all the details myself, but I know Jonathan Archer has issues. With me."

"Oh my goodness," Anna breathes over the phone. She sounds panicked. "You really think he took her?"

"Where are you now?"

"Outside the police station."

"Tell the police everything you told me. Everything you can think of that might help them find Jack as soon as possible," I say. "I'll talk to the detectives here."

"I'm so sorry, Emma. If I had known... I wish I could have done more."

"You've helped more than you know."

I hang up the phone, and head outside, looking for Sanchez.

FIFTY-FIVE

Sanchez is huddled under the porch with other officers. It strikes me that she'd rather be in a falling downpour than be in a room with me. She's disappointed in the way I handled the phone call with Anna, but I'm hoping this second call will restore her faith in me.

"I need to talk to you," I say.

"Not now." She's tapping away at her phone. Doesn't even look in my direction. "We're in the middle of something."

"It's about Anna."

At this, she lowers her hands, lifts her head and sighs.

"I already know about Anna. We sent officers to her location."

"She called me back."

This, Sanchez wasn't expecting me to say. "When?"

"Just now. She told me Jack has been acting suspicious all night. He lied to investigators about when he left the pumpkin patch."

"If that's the case, why didn't she come forward with this information sooner?"

"Because she didn't believe he could have anything to do

with the kidnapping. It wasn't until we started questioning her that she began to worry," I say. "She says she doesn't know where Claire or Jack are. I believe her."

Sanchez looks back at her phone. "I'm not sure how what she told you helps. She's likely saying the same thing to officers at the station as we speak. I'll allow them to decide whether she's telling the truth."

I ignore the last comment, focusing instead on the other information Anna provided.

"It means there's enough linking Jack to Claire's disappearance. He was at the scene. He's familiar with Claire, which means she would trust him. He lied about his whereabouts, and now no one can find him. And he's connected to David's accident two years ago," I say. "He took Claire."

There's a pause. Sanchez looks at me with the same sympathetic eyes that greeted me at the house this evening. She looks at me as a fellow human, a fellow mother. Then, just as quickly, she returns to business, looking at her phone.

"We agree. Jack Fox is likely the person who took your daughter." She pauses. "We just heard back from the officers with Katy Callaway. They questioned her again. It took some time, but she finally admitted Jack was the person who led her to the cornfields."

I gasp, an image of another child put in danger. "What did she say? Did he threaten her?"

"No. Actually, she said he told her some of the students were playing a special game of hide and seek. He told her to stay in the cornfields as long as she could if she wanted to win," she says. "And you were right about the soda. He gave it to her."

I think back to the way Katy reacted when I found her. She wasn't thinking about a game or keeping secrets. She was very, very scared. After being alone in the cornfields for so long, I wonder if she'd forgotten why she was there in the first place, or if Jack did threaten her, and she's too afraid to say.

"We're putting all our efforts into finding him," Sanchez says. "Which is why we're preparing to share his photo with the media."

"You're doing what?"

"Within twenty minutes, everyone in the area will no longer only be looking for Claire. They'll be looking for Fox, too."

"What happened to keeping our information under wraps? Using it to our advantage?"

"We're running out of time. The more people we have looking for Jack, the better our chances are of bringing Claire home."

"But this isn't a typical kidnapping case. Jack's motives are personal. If he hears his name on the radio... sees his picture on the news... he could end up doing something irrational. He could harm Claire."

"This is my choice to make—"

"But it's the wrong one!" I shout. Sure, Sanchez has more experience than I do when it comes to tackling crime, but I know Claire. And I know Jack. Maybe the latter isn't true, but I at least understand his motives. Taking Claire is about reclaiming what he's lost. If he realizes his plan is in jeopardy... I'm afraid of what he might do.

"Please," I beg. "Just give us more time to find Jack. I don't want anything pressuring him to make a rash decision."

"There are no easy choices in a situation like this," she says. "We still don't have all the information we want, but the more people we have looking, the better."

With that, she turns her back to me, continuing her conversation with the other officer. I try to listen to what she's telling him, but the rain pattering against the metal-roofed deck is loud. All my senses are in overdrive, it seems. I realize there's nothing left for me to do here. A decision has been made.

I turn to go back inside.

FIFTY-SIX

Any faith I had that I might be able to help in getting Claire back is gone.

Sanchez has decided I'm no longer an asset. I should trust in her background and experience, but everything inside me is telling me it's a mistake to release Jack's picture to the press. Admitting we know about him is dangerous.

As I told her, this isn't a typical kidnapping case, where a non-custodial parent is asserting his rights, or a twisted psychopath has lost control of his impulses.

Claire's kidnapping is personal. It's a way for Jack to take back just a little of what he has lost.

The heat of the living room is unbearable, an invisible wall almost stopping me in my tracks, but I keep walking.

"What happened?" Steven asks, his voice somber.

Piper is quick on her feet. "Did Sanchez say anything?"

I ignore both of them, walking to the staircase. I slowly climb the steps, taking myself away from the chaos of the investigation. Instead of turning in the direction of my bedroom, I walk into Claire's room, taking in each detail for what feels like the last time. I'm saying goodbye to her things, since I can't say the words to her.

I lower myself onto her bed, wrapping my arms around her pillow, inhaling her lavender smell.

Even though I've lost what little control I had, I also feel like I'm understanding, for the first time, Jack's true intentions in all of this. In his decision to take Claire in the first place.

The night of the accident created a hole in my life; it must have had the same impact on him. I lost my husband that night, but it's not until now that I know what it is like to truly lose everything. To be left with nothing and no one. To have a head full of memories and a heart full of hope, but circumstances that refuse to cooperate.

I'm helpless, unable to change any of the events going on around me.

I've felt this way for the past eight hours, and it's enough to make me double over in anger and hate.

Jack has been living with this feeling for two years. He *did* lose everything then. His girlfriend. His child. And now he's making sure I know exactly how much pain he's been through, by forcing me to experience it.

"Emma?" Piper has pushed open the door. "You have to tell us what's going on."

I open my mouth, but no words come out, as though even my voice refuses to do what I want. I burrow my head into the pillow and release a cry.

There's movement on the bed. Piper is now sitting beside me, rubbing my back. Steven is with her. I listen as he closes the door.

"Something must have happened," he says. "I tried asking Detective Sanchez, but she refused to tell me anything."

I sniffle, trying to find composure. When I do speak, the words come out strained.

"Anna made it clear Jack is involved. She said he lied to the police about his whereabouts at the pumpkin patch, and she has no idea where he is."

"Is that why you're so upset?" Piper asks.

The entire tragedy of having a child abducted is beyond upsetting, but there were at least moments earlier when I clung to hope. Now, I have nothing.

"Sanchez agrees that Jack is the one behind the kidnapping. She's so confident, she's releasing his picture."

"They're making progress." Steven tries, and fails, to sound hopeful. "That should be a good thing, right?"

"Jack didn't take Claire on a whim. He's been building up to this. Planning. He's probably long gone by now."

"Maybe not—"

"Just stop!" I shout, sitting upright on the bed. "Stop trying to make me feel better about what's happening. It's over, don't you get that? Jack has no intention of being found or bringing Claire back. He's doing all of this to get back at me for what happened that night. For what happened to Christine."

"It was an accident! And you weren't even there."

"But I still have my daughter. I've been able to go on living, even when it's been hard. Jack lost everything. I didn't know what that was like," I say. "Until now."

"Taking Claire won't bring Christine back," he says.

"No, but it gives him back some of the control he lost."

It's frightening to think of how clear Jack's logic seems to me now. This afternoon, I couldn't wrap my mind around why anyone would want to take my daughter. And yet now, in my desperation and loss, it's starting to make sense.

"Jonathan was always controlling," Piper adds. "That was his biggest issue with Christine. I can see how her death pushed him even further over the edge."

"If that's his logic, he must be mentally ill," says Steven.

"That's what worries me. We're not dealing with a rational person. Jack took several measures to make sure his plan would go off without a hitch. If he thinks the police are onto him, he has nothing left to lose. He'll end up hurting Claire, even if he hasn't already."

The room is silent for what feels like hours. At last, I think the reality of the situation is setting in with both of them. There's not an easy solution, because the problem itself is so complicated. Jack isn't after money or fame or pleasure. He's trying to take back what he lost, and the only way he can do that is by taking Claire.

"Jonathan and Christine were from Whitaker, right?" Steven is trying to be practical. "Maybe he took Claire back to his hometown."

"He wouldn't do that. It would be too risky," I say.

"Just try thinking. You've known this man for over a year. Even in passing, he might have let something slip. Something that could give us an idea of where he is going and what he plans on doing," Steven urges, before looking to Piper. "And you've known him even longer. Where would he go?"

I remember my conversation with Anna during the pumpkin patch ride at McCallister's. She said that on one of their dates Jack took her to the Bluffs, a popular hiking destination.

"The Bluffs," I say, hurriedly. "Anna said he took her there. That it was his favorite spot in North Ridge. He could be hiding out there long enough for the tension to settle, before leaving."

Piper perks up at this detail, suddenly remembering something.

"That's how Christine knew this place," she says. "When they first started dating, they went camping here. I remember her talking about that place. The Bluffs. She was so smitten with the town, she thought this would be a good place to start over."

"The Bluffs would be a good place to hide," Steven says. "It's remote. And every highway between here and the neighboring states will be blocked off. It would be too risky for him to make a lengthy car trip with a missing child."

"That's it. That's where he's taking Claire," I say, rushing out of the room and down the stairs, hoping this time Sanchez will hear what I have to say.

FIFTY-SEVEN

Night has fallen. Light shines from the porch, a weak yellow glow. When I walk outside, it takes several seconds for my eyes to adjust to the darkness. I squint at each face, searching for Sanchez.

"Where is the detective?" I ask, directing my question to a trio of officers leaning against the railing.

"She left," one answers, without looking up.

"Where did she go?"

"Not at liberty to say," the same officer responds.

"Can you tell me anything? I might have something that can help."

The first officer who spoke looks at me now.

"We've been told not to share any sensitive information about the investigation," he says. "When we hear back from the detective, you'll be the first to know."

I've clearly been deemed useless. The lack of control I have is overwhelming. It's my daughter that's been taken, and no one will even allow me to help. Of course, after my conversation with Anna, Sanchez believes I'm only impeding the investigation.

I stomp back into the house.

"What did Sanchez say?" Steven asks.

"She's not here."

"Where is she?" asks Piper.

"They won't tell me." I glare at the front door. "They're no longer listening to anything I have to say."

Steven starts walking to the door. "I'll talk to someone. If Jack is hiding out at the Bluffs, we have to let someone know."

"They're not listening, Steven! Their priority is getting Jack's picture to the media. The way they see it, enough time has been wasted and they're treating this like any other child abduction," I say. "But this is different. This is personal."

"We have to do something," Piper says. "The more I think about Jonathan being behind this, the worse I feel about what he might do."

"If the police show up at the Bluffs, it could turn dangerous." My head whirls with the possibilities. "We don't know if Jack has a gun. We don't know what he plans on doing. What if there is a shootout and Claire is lost in the crossfire?"

"What do you think he wants?" Steven asks.

I think about it. Jack's motives. His loss.

"He wants to take back the life that was stolen from him."

"Hurting Claire won't accomplish any of that," Piper says.

"I know. He may not want to hurt her, but if the police track him down, I'm afraid that's what will happen. The police won't reason with him." I pause, an idea forming. "But I will."

"What are you suggesting?" asks Steven.

"What if I could get to Jack and Claire before the police do? What if I can talk to him?"

"You can't be serious," Piper says. "That's way too risky."

"But it could be safer for Claire. If the police show up, Jack will know he's already lost the battle. If I'm there, maybe I could at least reason with him."

Piper shakes her head. She looks at Steven for help. "Tell her this is ridiculous."

"Maybe it's not. Emma is right. Everything Jack has done ties back to the night of the car accident. If Emma confronts him, tells him she understands why he did all of this, it might de-escalate the situation."

"No! You're both out of your minds."

"What other choice do we have?" I ask. "We can't just wait on the police to release the photo. For a nationwide manhunt to begin. That will put too much pressure on Jack, and he might have no choice but to do something dangerous. Either that, or enough time passes that he leaves town with Claire, never to be seen again. At least this way we have an opportunity to do something."

"How are you going to get to the Bluffs?" she asks.

"The police are ignoring me," I say. "I could find a way out of the house."

"Or I could take you," Steven says. "I'm not letting you go alone. David would never want me to do that."

"We'll need a plan," Piper says, at last.

"I haven't left the house all night. I'll tell the police I'm leaving to get us food," Steven says.

"And I can sneak out the back. I'll run down the street and meet up with you there."

"What am I supposed to do?" Piper asks.

"You stay here in case the police start asking questions. They won't be suspicious if they have eyes on at least one of us. You can tell them Emma is resting upstairs."

"And if this doesn't work, then what? You could show up at the Bluffs and no one is there."

"It's better than sitting around here and waiting. I must do something to get my daughter back."

I'm not convinced confronting Jack on my own is the right

decision, but I think it's the best one considering my limited options. If I'm certain about one thing, it's that we shouldn't treat Jack like a typical child abductor. His motives are more complicated than that, and I'm the only person that can understand them.

FIFTY-EIGHT

I'm out of breath. The adrenaline pumping through my veins has my heart working in overdrive.

As promised, Piper wandered to the front of the house to keep the officers distracted. No one saw me as I slipped off the back porch and started running in the direction of the street, but I'm still worried one of them will catch onto what we're doing.

A car slows at the stop sign where Steven and I agreed to meet. As I approach, I see him behind the wheel.

"Are you sure about this?"

I'm already sliding into the passenger seat. "Did the cops give you a hard time about leaving?"

"No. They seemed distracted."

"Do you think they've already released Jack's photo to the press?"

"I haven't checked," he says, merging the car onto the highway. "If Jack is at the Bluffs, he won't have service, so that works in our favor."

I'm not sure if that's true. It's good that Jack won't be able to check for updates, but it also means we won't have a way of contacting the police if we find ourselves in danger.

"I don't think there will be more rain tonight, but the grounds will be slick," Steven says. "We'll have to watch our step."

It's obvious he's nervous, trying to talk about anything other than what we're about to do.

"You should probably stay with the car. If something goes wrong, at least you'll be able to drive to town and get help."

"I already told you, I'm not letting you do this alone." He tightens his grip around the steering wheel. "I owe this to David. I need to keep you both safe."

David would be proud of his brother tonight, proud of the man he's become in the past two years. Steven is no longer the selfish person he was on the night of David's accident. He's putting others' needs before his own, choosing to do what is right instead of what is easy.

"How are you feeling about Piper?" I ask. "It can't be easy, knowing she lied about the real reason she came to North Ridge."

"It isn't." His grip on the steering wheel tightens. "Her sole reason for coming here was to get to know me. Neither of us knew we'd end up falling in love."

"You are in love though, right? She couldn't fake that."

"I love her," he says, pausing. "I love her so much I want to believe her. Grief does things to people. Maybe she was afraid telling me about Christine would ruin what we had built together."

"It's hard feeling like even the happy parts of your life are touched by sadness. Maybe that's why she never told you. She didn't want you to think about the accident every time you were with her."

"It's a conversation we'll have. After we bring Claire home. If she cared about Christine half as much as I did for David, then I know she's living with this pain, too."

We don't talk the rest of the way to the Bluffs. The drive

turns quieter and darker as the car moves closer to the wilderness.

"Look ahead," Steven says.

In front of us, there is a car pulled to the side of the road.

"Does that look like the rental car?"

"I don't know. But at least we know we're not alone."

I get out of the car and inspect the vehicle. It's abandoned.

"He probably left the car here so he could hike deeper into the woods and set up camp," Steven says. "It's a good place to avoid people if he's waiting to leave town."

"We need to search the area. See if we can find their campsite."

"There are miles of wilderness out here. We could search for days and still not find them."

"They can't be that far ahead of us. An hour, two hours, at most. Besides, if he left the car here, he couldn't have gone too far."

We hike through the forest, using only our cell phones to guide our way. It still feels like we're in complete darkness. I can hardly make out trees in front of me, and every snap of brush beneath my feet makes me jump.

"Stop," Steven whispers, and I freeze. "Look ahead."

Through the darkness, I'm able to catch a glimpse of light. It's a small campfire.

"Someone is there."

And then I hear a sound. A small, human sound. Someone is crying.

"I'm scared," the voice says. *Claire*.

"It's okay," another voice says. "I'm not going to hurt you."

It's Jack. They're here.

FIFTY-NINE

It wasn't supposed to be like this.

It was supposed to be the start of a great adventure. A new life together. The Plan.

I took careful steps to prepare everything. I bought stuffed animals and a pink sleeping bag with a unicorn on the front. I'd hoped when she woke up, she'd be surprised, happy. But Claire won't stop crying. Won't stop complaining. She's cold. Hungry. Scared.

My heart starts beating faster. I'd thought I'd planned for everything, but now I'm alone in the forest with a little girl, and I don't know what to do.

"I want to go home," Claire says.

"We're going someplace better than home. We can go anywhere you want." I kneel in front of her, meeting her at eye level. "Tell me where you want to go, yeah? We can stay in the woods. Go to the beach. Move to a big city and live in one of those tall skyscrapers. Don't you see how exciting this is? We get the chance to start over."

I keep my voice light and animated, like I'm reading a children's book, trying to stir some excitement, but she only looks confused. She stares at the animals and blanket I've brought her like they're coiling snakes.

So, I try a different method, something that will remind her I'm doing this for her as much as I'm doing it for me. I rummage through my knapsack, pulling out the picture I'd stolen from Laura's classroom earlier this week.

It's a drawing Claire made the first week of school. A drawing of her family. I'd already been working on The Plan for a while, but once I saw this, I was convinced I was making the right decision. Claire had lost her father, and it was my mission to give her a new one.

"Do you remember making this, Claire?" I ask, unfolding the picture. I point at the angel floating in the sky. Her father. "Do you know who that is?"

But Claire won't answer. She only cries harder.

"I'm trying to make you understand," I say, in my most soothing tone. "I can be your father now. We can start over with a new family. Just the two of us. I'll take care of you, just like you were my own."

"I want my mommy," she cries.

"No! No, you don't!" I shout.

My voice echoes in the forest, startling even me. All this work, all this planning... and she doesn't appreciate any of it. This girl is so ungrateful. She doesn't realize how lucky she is to have a second chance. Her father is gone, but I'm here now. What's been taken from her has been returned, and all she wants is Emma.

Christine would have been such a wonderful mother... far better than Emma. She wouldn't run herself ragged with work and other responsibilities. She would have turned all her attention to me and our child. The life we could have built together would have been complete. Beautiful.

Claire is wrapped up in the sleeping bag. Her cries have stopped. My shouting scared her.

"I'm sorry I yelled," I say. "It's been a long day. Let me give you something to drink."

I take the chocolate milk carton and add a few more drops of the sleeping serum, giving the liquid a stir with the plastic straw.

"Get some rest. You'll feel better in the morning."

She takes a few sips and settles down.

"We won't be here long," I say, taking the drink. "I promise."

SIXTY

EMMA

We're now close enough to see a small tent and a pile of wood by the fire. Jack's back is to us. I can't see Claire, but I hear her voice, so I know she's there.

"Jack?"

He stands quickly, and when he turns, I can see he's holding a knife in his hand. He's using it to strip wood, but when he sees us, he points the blade at Claire.

"No!" I scream.

"Mommy!" Claire's panic almost matches mine.

It's startling how our voices carry.

"What are you doing here, Emma?" Jack asks.

"I'm bringing my daughter home."

"How did you...? Why are you...?"

"You need to stop this, Jack," Steven says. "It's over."

"No, it's not. Claire and I are going to leave here. Start a new life together."

To anyone listening, Jack sounds deranged, disconnected from reality. And yet, I understand what he wants. It's what I want, too. To recapture the lives we had before that awful night, as impossible as that may be.

"I know your real name is Jonathan Archer," I begin. "And I know about Christine."

"But you don't care, do you? If you knew anything about her, you would have been able to identify me a long time ago. But you didn't. For months, we've worked alongside each other, and you never knew because you didn't care."

"I do care. I never looked into it before because I was in pain, too. We both lost something that night."

"No. You lost something. I lost *everything*. Your husband died. I know how much that must have hurt. But me? I lost my girlfriend and our child. In one instant, my entire future changed. You at least had the option to pick up the pieces. You had your daughter. What did I have? Nothing."

"What happened that night wasn't anyone's fault—" Steven starts.

"The hell it wasn't! I know exactly who to blame." He looks at me. "It was your husband. David."

"What happened that night wasn't David's fault. And it wasn't Christine's fault either—"

"Then who am I supposed to blame?" he screams. "I can't keep going through life with all this anger."

"Blame me!" I shout back. "I'm the person at fault."

Everyone is silent, waiting for me to continue. I'm wrestling with a truth I promised to never speak aloud, but now it feels like my only choice.

"I got into an argument with my husband that day. I was being selfish. The only reason he was on the road that night is because of me."

Steven looks to me. "No, that's not what happened. I got into a fight with David."

I'm crying now, my mind being pulled between the tragedy of the past and the terror of the present.

"He wanted us to all go home together, but I started a fight over something ridiculous, and he left. He went to a store and bought art supplies because he was trying to make *me* happy. That's why he was late getting home. That's why he was on the road when the accident happened." I look at Steven. "I'm the reason he died."

Steven looks away. I'm not sure whether my admission provides him relief or more sadness. When he does speak, he looks past me, his gaze landing on Jack. "There was a storm that night. It was an accident."

"No, it wasn't!" Jack screams. "Christine didn't deserve for her life to end that way. And I don't deserve to be alone the rest of my life, either. That's why I have Claire. The two of us can start over somewhere, and it will be like nothing happened."

Claire makes a small whimper.

"You're scaring her, Jack," I say. "We've both lost people we love. But think about what Claire has been through. She doesn't deserve to be traumatized because of our pain."

"She's only upset because you're here. You're not supposed to be here!"

"She's my little girl. She's all I have left. Think of her," I say. "Think of the child you lost."

"My child *was* taken." He winces. "We would have been perfect. Christine and me and the baby."

I've tried reasoning with him, tried apologizing, even spoken the truth about that night to try and make him understand. Perhaps, it's time Jack faces his own truth. Maybe that's the best way to resolve this.

"Jack, you're lying."

He raises his head, a strange look on his face. "What are you talking about?"

"Christine was here because she was leaving you, Jack. That's why she left Whitaker."

"How do you...? Why are you saying this?"

"She didn't even tell you about the baby."

He's wiping his brow, as if the truth is just now coming back to him. "You don't know anything. You didn't know Christine."

"I talked to her friend, Piper. She told me everything. That Christine wanted to start over *away* from you. She may have wanted the baby, but she had no desire to raise a child with you."

"Piper?" His confusion grows. "That's just not true. It's a lie."

"Christine wouldn't have wanted any of this." My desperation and exhaustion are taking over. I'm running out of words. "Please, don't destroy my family to try and recreate one that never even existed."

"Stop lying!"

He charges at me, but before he can reach me, Steven barrels at him with full force. He tackles him to the ground and the two men scuffle, the knife falling from both their grasps. Jack wriggles away first. When he gets to his feet, instead of lunging for the weapon, he takes off running, in the direction of the woods.

SIXTY-ONE

The Plan isn't working.

It was a stupid plan to begin with, but what else can you ask of a broken man?

If Christine were here, so much would be different. I'd never feel alone. I'd never feel the urge to take out my anger on others.

"Hey, stop!"

The man who came with Emma is chasing after me. I don't even know who he is, and I don't care. I continue running through the night, as though if I try hard enough, I might be able to run back in time, be with my family once again.

They're supposed to be here with me. At this very spot. We would have had a wedding by now. A house built, overlooking the Bluffs. Our baby would be walking. In my dreams, I always picture a son. I would have named him after me. We would have called him Jack.

"Slow down," the man chasing me shouts.

Emma's words worm their way into my mind. Claiming Christine didn't want me or our life together.

I think back to that night, our phone call before the line went dead, right before the accident that took her life. I worked so hard to block it out.

"It's over, Jack," she said. "I never planned on telling you about the baby."

"It's our baby. My baby."

"You control everything I say and do. That's not a life. Not one I want for our child."

"You don't have a choice, Christine. We have a life together. You can't just walk away!"

She was getting upset, crying harder. "Please let me go."

"I'll never let you go. Or the baby. Wherever you go, I'll find you. You can't stop me—"

Then silence. I never heard her sweet voice again.

"You're getting too close to the cliffs," the man behind me shouts. "It's dangerous out here!"

I know how dangerous the world can be. I imagine Dr. Meade, lying dead and bloody beside a basement staircase. Then I picture Christine, feeling as though her only shot at happiness was a life without me.

I trip and fall, landing hard on my stomach. My chest hurts as I try to inhale. I reach my arms forward, but there is no ground beneath them. I've reached the cliff's edge, the spot that gives the Bluffs its name.

"Be careful." *The man has caught up to me. He's standing back, nervously.* "It's dark."

I've been living in darkness for too long. I stand, shakily. The wind whips past my face, pulling me in one direction, my instincts pulling me in another.

I take a step forward.

My arms are outstretched.

Reaching for Christine.

Reaching for my child.

Reaching... reaching...

SIXTY-TWO

EMMA

I kneel in front of the fire, scooping Claire into my arms.

I'd heard her voice only moments ago, but now it looks like she's sleeping. Did he hurt her, and I didn't see?

"Claire, honey. I'm here."

She moves. "Mommy?"

I pull her close to me, warm tears running down my cheeks. I'm smiling, so relieved to have her with me again.

"I'm here, honey. Everything is okay. You're safe."

"I'm cold," she says.

"I know. We'll leave here soon. I promise."

The sound of someone approaching. Fear returns. I pull her closer to me. When the man comes closer, I'm able to see Steven. The fear settles.

"Is Jack...?"

Before I can finish my question, Steven shakes his head. Whatever happened out there, it doesn't matter. All I need to know is that we're all safe.

Steven kneels beside the fire. He wraps his arms around us.

"I'm so happy you're safe, Claire Bear," he says.

Claire Bear. It's a nickname her father gave her when she

was a baby. I'd forgotten it. I've forgotten so many of the happy moments, focusing only on the unhappy one we shared right before his death.

I miss David. I have missed him, and I'll continue to miss him for the rest of my life. But I can't push his memory away, otherwise my grief will consume me, as it did with Jack.

Maybe it's the emotional intensity of the moment, or my exhausted mind playing tricks on me, but I can almost feel David here with us. With Claire in my arms, his spirit around us, I feel complete.

"Let's take you home," I tell my darling girl.

SIXTY-THREE

ONE YEAR LATER

Ribbons are tied around every present. Some are pink, some are blue. Steven and Piper have decided they'll learn the gender in the delivery room. In only a few more weeks, they'll know whether they're bringing home a little boy or a little girl.

The baby shower is being held at their three-story house on the other end of town. In the past year, this place has become like a second home to us. Since Claire returned, we've been almost inseparable from Piper and Steven, and Claire is relishing in the fact she'll soon have a baby cousin.

"Claire Bear, want to hand over the next present?"

She quickly runs across the room, grabbing a small box from the pile, and brings it over to her aunt. Piper has reached the uncomfortable stage of pregnancy where she prefers to move as little as possible. Claire is happy to play assistant.

"I'm not sure who is more excited to meet the baby," Steven says. "Claire or me."

Steven and I are standing toward the back of the room. Most of the guests have visited North Ridge from Piper's home-town, and I think we both feel a little out of place around them.

"There's nothing like holding your child in your arms for the first time," I tell him. "It's something that will change you."

Steven looks around. "Don't tell Piper, but I'm getting a little scared."

"That's natural. You have nothing to worry about. You'll be a great father."

I don't elaborate on the fact that fear comes hand-in-hand with parenting. The love, the worry, the instinct to protect. It's all combined. I think Steven understands that more than most new fathers, given what he experienced with us the day Claire was taken.

"How is she doing with... everything?"

"Better. She's been sleeping in her room more and more," I say. "I'm the one still struggling. On the nights she's not beside me, I check her room at least a dozen times."

"I'd say that's natural, too."

I'm grateful Claire was unconscious for most of the hours she spent with Jonathan Archer. She only woke up at the campsite, and even then, her memories are hazy. Nothing really registers beyond knowing Jack was there, and Steven and I arrived soon after.

For me, every emotion from that day is committed to memory. I try to focus on the good part, the happy ending. But it's frightening to admit how close I came to losing my daughter forever. If we hadn't acted quickly enough, she could have slipped away never to be seen again. Or worse, Jonathan Archer's instability could have gotten the best of both of them.

I think of him a lot, too. The papers all refer to him by his given name, but in my mind, he's still Jack. The young man I worked alongside for almost a year, never knowing his plot to destroy my life. Most people that talk about the incident comment on how deranged he was, but, if I'm being honest, I'm more startled by the similarities in our lives.

We both lost people we loved the night of the car accident,

and we allowed that loss to change us for the worse. We both pushed people away. I kept Piper and Steven at a distance, determined to prove to them and to David and myself I could handle everything on my own, even when I couldn't.

Jack always claimed to be alone, but that wasn't true. He had people who were willing to help him, too. If only he'd let them in. He had Anna. She didn't know about his life before North Ridge, about his loss, but I trust that if she did, she would have helped him through it.

And he had his therapist, Dr. Meade. Apparently, she'd worked with him extensively in the months since Christine's death, trying to help him manage his grief. She'd written multiple essays about his experience and their progress together. She considered him one of her greatest success stories; unfortunately, she didn't know the severity of his mental decline until it was too late.

Jack had people willing to listen, willing to help. He pushed them away, leaving him alone with his dark thoughts, and it ruined him.

I don't want to end up like him, which is why I've changed.

I no longer keep my memories of David at a distance, and I've forgiven myself for the mistakes I made. What happened to David and Christine was an accident. Jack, Steven and I all had different roles to play, but none of us caused what happened, and I've accepted that. Steven knows about my argument with David and his spontaneous trip to the store, but he doesn't hold it against me. We all have moments in our past we wish to change, but all we can really control is our actions in the present.

"Looks like that's all the gifts," Piper says, clasping her hands together. "Thank you all for your generosity."

"Let's get a picture of the parents-to-be!" someone in the crowd shouts.

"I guess that's my cue," Steven says, moving closer to Piper.

After posing for several pictures, Piper waves over to Claire. "Let's take one more with the whole family," she says.

Steven beckons to me. "That means you, Emma."

I walk to the front of the room and stand beside Steven. Claire stands in front of us, holding my hand.

"I love you, Mommy," she whispers, before facing the camera.

"I love you more, my darling girl," I say back.

The four of us look at the camera and smile. A family reunited. All that's missing is her father, and yet, I feel him with us in every happy moment.

If I've learned anything in the years since David died, it's that all families are broken, but the best ones find a way to come back together.

A LETTER FROM MIRANDA

Dear reader,

Thank you for taking the time to read *The School Trip*. If you liked it and want information about upcoming releases, sign up with the following link. Your email address will never be shared and you can unsubscribe at any time.

www.bookouture.com/miranda-smith

I've shared the book's premise with a few people, and they all agree this story is every parent's, and every teacher's, worst nightmare. Although the idea for *The School Trip* came to me while I was chaperoning a field trip, I've always felt welcomed and secure at local school events. I'm grateful for the amazing educators in my life and in the lives of my children. Teachers go above and beyond to nurture and protect future generations, yet are often underappreciated. If you're a teacher and you're reading this, thank you for all you do!

If you'd like to discuss any of my books, I'd love to connect! You can find me on Facebook, Twitter and Instagram, or my website. If you enjoyed *The School Trip*, I'd appreciate it if you left a review on Amazon. It only takes a few minutes and does wonders in helping readers discover my books for the first time.

Thank you again for your support!

Sincerely,

Miranda Smith

www.mirandasmithwriter.com

facebook.com/MirandaSmithAuthor

twitter.com/msmithbooks

instagram.com/mirandasmithwriter

ACKNOWLEDGMENTS

I'd like to thank the people at Bookouture for their support and encouragement, especially Sarah Hardy, Jane Eastgate and Liz Hurst. Thank you to Ruth Tross, my fabulous editor. I so enjoy working with you on these crazy, twisted stories.

I'd like to thank Retired Detective Jason Oury for sharing his own experiences and speaking with me about the police procedures mentioned in this book. All mistakes are completely my own.

I'd like to thank the loyal readers, reviewers and bloggers for being so very supportive and helping to promote each new book. It's because of you I'm able to continue writing.

Much love goes out to my family: my parents, Bonnie and Fud, my sisters, husband and children. I love you all very much. This book is dedicated to Christopher, the baby of our family. I'm thankful for each day I get to watch you learn and grow. I love you.

Made in the USA
Middletown, DE
16 July 2024